D0731415

Southwest Corner Stories

by Floyd McCracken

SHASTA VALLEY PRESS

ACKNOWLEDGEMENTS

This book is based on columns published in The San Diego Union in the years between 1962 and 1975.

The columns have been selected and edited for reprinting in book form by Phil McCracken, the author's son.

Illustrations are by Jim Burnett and the late Bob Fassett, San Diego Union staff artists, and by Todd Weaver, great-grandson of the author.

Cover design by John Signor.

Copyright 1993, Phil McCracken

Published by Shasta Valley Press
Printed in the U.S.A.

Library of Congress catalog card number:
98-85273
ISBN: 0-9637445-7-7

FOREWORD

*F*loyd McCracken was a wordsmith. He loved words. He savored them. He respected them. For him the ability to use words represented a way to escape the hardships of a homesteader's life in the Pacific Northwest.

In a career that spanned more than 42 years, Floyd McCracken served as a reporter, editorial writer and editor of newspapers from Seattle to San Diego.

Born in a dirt floor log cabin in 1891, Mr. McCracken never lost sight of his humble beginnings as a homesteader's son. In the years after he retired at the age of 70, he wrote more than 700 columns for The San Diego Union. They were based on memories of his boyhood years and his experiences as a newsman.

His commentaries, and those of other staff writers, appeared in the lower left corner of The Union's editorial page — *The Southwest Corner*. The columns covered a wide range of subjects from homesteading to interesting personalities and places.

Floyd McCracken grew up to respect authority, honesty, homespun humor, thrift and hard work. His writings reflect those ideals. The following pages are a collection of his recollections — the best of Floyd's *Southwest Corner* stories.

CONTENTS

The Homestead Years

People And Places

The Homestead Years

JIM BURNETT

I Never Knew Poverty

R ecently I have come to believe that I personally never knew poverty. This surprises me a little because I have lived through hard times, business declines, recessions, and depressions. We knew them by different names, but they all had about the same effect upon human hopes and realizations.

But poverty — no. In my younger days the word seldom was used, and I think there was a good reason.

To have applied the word to conditions of our society would have been to admit defeat, and that we were not about to do.

There were other reasons, too. Men were willing and eager to work at any honorable task that would earn a little money. They had an abiding sense of responsibility for their families. I knew a man (my father) who worked in the woods, making fence rails and posts. He got a dollar for 100 rails and the same amount for 150 posts, but he had to take half of his pay in wheat. The grain was taken to a mill 3 miles away where it was ground into flour, the miller taking half of the wheat for his pay.

Today that man and his family doubtless would be classed as poverty stricken, but I am sure he would have rejected any such idea with scorn. Tomorrow would be better, he told himself. He would make it better.

It is true that some things were simpler in those days. The clothing we wore was truly functional. A couple of pairs of overalls (with the pockets riveted in), rough work shirts, laced boots, and a hat. These were standard for man and boy. Underwear was for winter.

I Never Knew Poverty

Father could repair just about anything, from boots to harness and wagon wheels.

Food, too, was simple. Plenty of bread, sometimes butter, occasionally beef or venison that was boiled or fried, stewed chicken, smoked ham and bacon from our own smokehouse, beans, cooked cereal for breakfast — such fare was filling if not fancy. Cakes and pies were for Sunday or holidays.

There would be jams and jellies if the wild huckleberries had done well, or if currants and gooseberries had produced a good crop. We raised our own potatoes, carrots, and cabbage. These were stored in frost-resistant root houses for winter use.

I have a notion that such conditions today would cause a political storm. There would be an outcry that would reach across the land. Relief would be forthcoming, and I am not saying this would not be a good thing.

I am saying the life we lived inspired a code of self-reliance. Because there was no other way, we learned to meet adversity with a belief that we would conquer.

And another thing — we never were overwhelmed with a lack of mental stimulation. There was no poverty of the mind. The few books we had were read and reread.

The odd thing about all that is that we were struggling toward what we have today.

(Editor's Note: This column was published in The Union on Jan. 3, 1966 and was entered into the Congressional Record on Feb. 17, 1966.)

A Tribute to Haywire

*L*et me join any who would write a poem or a song dedicated to baling wire, popularly known as haywire.

My hat is off to Carl Hayden, writer for the Boise, Idaho, Statesman, who has a sense of values and a long memory.

He does not venture into the fields of poetry or song writing, but in paying tribute to this item that helped win the West, he does know his haywire.

Without this strand of metal there are many things that could not have been conquered or developed.

Haywire primarily was for binding bales of hay, but much of it never saw a bale. It could be purchased at any hardware store. It came in heavy rolls and was sold by the pound.

It was used and reused. Salvaged from bales of timothy and clover, and later from alfalfa, it became the greatest unsung aid in the conquest of the West. There seemed to be nothing that could not be mended with the wire.

Repairs nearly always were regarded as temporary, but rarely was the wire replaced.

We mended broken harness with haywire. We bound up weak wagon tongues with the wire. I have wound cracked ax handles so neatly with haywire that no other repairs ever were necessary.

I have known ranchers to pause while fixing a fence (with haywire, of course) to use a piece of wire to hold suspenders and trousers together after a button had given way.

In the house we repaired broken skillet handles, strengthened chair legs and reinforced bedsteads

5

with haywire. Even today, a hundred or more years after "temporary repairs" were made, antique dealers still find pieces of furniture and household utensils bound tightly with wire.

Once I went hunting with a 10-gauge shotgun that would not fire without a loop of wire around the barrel to hold it in position for the firing pin to strike the cap in the shell.

In time haywire became a slightly derogatory term. A rundown or wornout ranch or business was known as a "haywire operation."

But many such outfits or operations did magnificent service.

Long live haywire!

How to Find a Bee Tree

While I don't suppose hunting bee trees is a popular pursuit, it is just possible someone might want to know how it is done.

In bygone days a bee tree was highly prized in Oregon's Willamette Valley, and well worth going after.

The honey makers were known as little black bees, or wild bees. Although ferocious in the defense of home and honey, they seemed to follow a philosophy of "let me alone and I'll let you alone."

They had no hives, but they had homes, mostly in hollow trees where they stored the fruits of their labor. They could be induced to work in a hive, if a man had the courage to corral them.

Usually the presence of a bee tree was indicated when a large number of bees were in the air or working among the wild flowers and tree blossoms.

For several days the observer would note the direction of flight as the bees came for nectar, or departed with loads. The bees usually flew straight from the tree to the flowers, but on departure for the tree they circled a little then took a "bee line" for home.

The honey-hungry watcher noted the direction of flight.

Then he moved perhaps 100 yards to his right

or left, noting the flight of the workers. He now had two lines that would converge at or near the tree. When he had followed these lines to their meeting point he was on target.

Sometimes the bees were lodged in a towering Douglas fir high above the ground. It took a keen eye to see them as they entered or left their home, but having detected bee activity the honey hunter was ready for action.

Enlisting the aid of a neighbor, he felled the tree, trying to avoid breaking it. A broken bee tree meant loss of much of the honey.

After the tree crashed to earth the men hurried along the trunk with a smoke pot to discourage the angry swarm. They plugged the entrance to the colony's hoard and then turned their attention to fighting off the militant bees.

Sometimes they were able to capture the queen and lead the bees into a hive.

The honey harvesters sawed through the tree above and below where they believed the deposit to be, then carefully split the tree open.

Often a couple of tubs of honey would be gathered. Much of it was mixed with decayed wood and comb from the inside of the tree. That problem would be solved by warming it and filtering it through clean curtain material. Some of it might be three or four years old.

It was good, especially on a stack of flapjacks. Was it better than today's carefully packaged product? Perhaps not. But gathering it was more exciting than reaching for a jar on the grocer's shelf.

1899: Unlimited Trees

I was a small boy when it happened, around 8 or 9 years old, so I don't blame myself. Nor do I blame my father. He was doing the best he knew, and everyone at that time thought the Northwest had a limitless supply of timber.

It was a simple matter; the railroad that ran nearby needed wood to fuel its steam locomotives. There was no other work for strong men with families to feed.

So father took a contract one winter to cut 400 cords of Oregon's finest Douglas fir into 30-inch lengths and deliver it to the side of the tracks three miles away.

The timber he cut had grown thick and tall on rolling hills about 10 miles south of Salem. It was so dense almost no understory grew. Trees were so close together that fallers used great care lest one falling giant lodge against another.

It was grueling work. The long cross-cut saws were aptly named "misery whips." On days when weather was favorable, father and his little crew cut and limbed trees. When rain fell they stretched a piece of 24-foot canvas over a fallen giant. It was wide enough for the men to stand under and pull their one-man saws without getting too wet.

The timber was prime, meaning it did not have doty, or rotten, spots. Every stick had to be sound. Furthermore, no part of the tree less than 20 inches in diameter could be used. Thus much good timber was left in the woods — timber that builders today would trade their eye-teeth for.

The wood had to be split, stacked and measured, then hauled to the railroad siding and stacked again. The railroad demanded a full 128 cubic feet of wood in each cord, and I am certain my dad gave a little extra. He was that kind of man.

As trains came through, they stopped by the corded wood and loaded their tenders.

Father bought the standing timber from a farmer named Matt Wood, who doubtless thought the land would be worth more to him if cleared for pasture. He had sheep, some cattle and hogs.

In recent years I visited the area and saw the land where that fine stand of timber had been. It really isn't very good pasture. The soil consists of a reddish clay that is more suited to growing trees than producing grass.

Indeed, I cannot escape the belief that it was meant to grow trees. (Feb. 26, 1970)

Clock Ticks Up Profit

*A*lthough my father never was a man to engage in big deals or to expect big profits, he made one investment that yielded a nine-fold profit. It began in the summer of 1898.

One of our neighbors near Salem, Ore., was selling his stock and personal property such as furniture and tools. He had arranged for an auction.

Such auctions were semi-social events. All the neighbors stopped work, if possible, and attended. There always was a lot of visiting. Usually someone, perhaps the auctioneer or his employer, provided sandwiches and coffee.

Father came home from the auction with a clock. It was an eight-day Seth Thomas time keeper that was supposed to strike the hour and the half hour. Mother took one look at it and said, "And what did you pay for that old wreck?"

"Twenty-five cents," father replied in that tone of voice long used by husbands who suddenly realize they may have made an error.

"Will it run? Will it keep good time? Why do we need another clock?"

"It won't run now, but I'll fix it," he replied.

And fix it he did.

The clock, not overly handsome, stood two feet tall on a shelf in the parlor. A glass door covered the front of the clock. The bottom half of the door bore a colored picture of a ring-neck pheasant standing on his toes as if ready to issue his clarion call.

After father had completed his ministrations, which included oiling, the clock began keeping time in our home, and it kept at it for 15 years.

The mechanism was powered by two iron

weights suspended on strings that wound around shafts. We wound those weights each Saturday night.

The first half of the week the clock ran about two minutes fast and the second half it lost about two minutes, thus bringing it back to correct time.

And faithfully it hammered on a musical gong each hour and each half hour.

After a few years we loaded a few things, including the old clock, into a wagon and moved to northern Idaho where father took a homestead.

The clock accepted its new home without complaint, although in winter we always had to shorten the length of the pendulum a little. That made it tick a little faster and thus overcame the effects of the temperature-thickened oil on the gears.

Finally came the day when father held his own auction. He had decided to leave the homestead and move into a town where there were better schools.

At first he doubted that anyone would buy the clock, but his auctioneer insisted on making a try.

And he sold it — for $2.50. Percentage wise, that probably was the biggest deal father ever made.

Mother's Feather Bed

Since, to my knowledge, no one has written an essay about the feather bed, I feel an irresistible urge to do so.

This lowly symbol of pioneering affluence once was the pride and joy of every person who could acquire one.

After the custom of her time, my mother made and brought one to the frugal home into which she married.

When Mother set out to make that mattress of feathers, she wisely bought heavy, closely woven tick- ing that might be called canvas today. She hand- sewed the material to make a bag large enough to cover a double bed.

Grandmother kept a flock of great white geese on the family's Indiana farm. She helped her daughter pluck feathers from the flock, an operation the geese protested loudly, though they need not have been alarmed. The feathers were due to fall out anyway.

I don't recall how many feathers it required, but it runs in my mind to have been 18 pounds.

That feather bed was something to behold.

The feathers were crush-resistant. A weary man could sleep on it night after night and the feathers would spring back into shape.

After long years of use, however, the feathers began to lose their resiliency.

We had no geese on our Idaho homestead, but

we had chickens. To fortify her precious feather bed, Mother sorted out the softer chicken feathers that became available after fat hens had joined a kettle of dumplings.

Those feathers were mixed in with the tired goose feathers. The original feathers never were quite the same after that.

How does it happen that, today, the term featherbedding does so little to pay tribute to this once-proud possession of the home?

Shopping Was Different

*I*n the time of my youth, when material poverty joined with spiritual wealth to form a way of life, shopping had a charm that no longer exists. It was "buying things at the store."

This shopping at the store routine was quite different from buying things through a mail-order catalogue, which has its charm, too. And the infrequent visits to the store were in marked contrast to the rush-in, try, fit, pay and rush-out again that characterizes today's sprees.

We bought only when the need no longer could be delayed. This made it imperative that price and quality be considered with great care. There was a devotion to money so pervasive you could almost touch it.

The merchants (we called them store-keepers) were well schooled to this situation. They knew they were going to sell; we had a minimum of rough shoes, shirts and overalls and our entry into a store was a confession that a replacement was necessary. And the merchants knew they would have to shave their prices a bit.

This led to a universal custom, in our area, at least, of placing a coded price mark on the merchandise. This code usually consisted of a series of letters from the alphabet, each letter standing for a numeral. The value of the letter was known only to the store clerks. A pair of shoes marked $2.50 would have this figure penciled on the price-tag, and above the figure would appear three letters. Thus the clerk could know what the shoes had cost wholesale and could shave the price a few cents, if that were necessary to make a sale.

Shopping Was Different

But my father had another method of getting value for his scarce dollars. First he would inspect the shoes critically, feeling the leather with his rough thumb and forefinger. He looked at the thickness of the soles, smelled the shoes to get an idea of the method used in tanning the leather. Putting a pair aside, he would take up another, going through the whole routine again.

When the try-on time came he would feel for roominess. Was there plenty of room for growing young feet?

The shoes were not bad, father would say finally. No, not bad, but it seemed the price was a mite steep. After all, $2.50 for a pair of shoes for a boy — and besides, the catalogue merchants had what appeared to be the same shoe for $2.25.

The storekeeper might cut a dime from his price, but sometimes he refused. Then father had another gimmick.

"OK," he'd say. "Throw in a pair of cotton socks or some shoelaces, and wrap them up."

It was a small victory, but father had prevailed.

From Rags to "Riches"

O ne of the most useful institutions in the Northern Idaho home of my youth was a rag bag. It commonly was a seamless sugar sack, but at times it may have been only a clean, standard-size grain sack.

Into this bag went every scrap of used cloth the home produced. It might have been the clean remnant of a pair of Levis, or a bit of cloth left over after mother had made a dress.

Out of the bag came scraps for mending. Also from it came an incident that gave us an undeserved reputation for being a "rich" family.

John and Lester were neighbor boys who watched in wonder as we unloaded our household effects on move-in day. Afterward they reported to another neighbor that we were rich; we had a carpet.

The carpet came circuitously from the rag bag.

Over several years mother had frugally saved all old garments and pieces of cloth that our home generated. Later, if those scraps were not needed for mending, they were sewed into inch-wide strips and wound into balls. Eventually we had several sacks of rag balls.

In those days there were a few operators who would weave the rags into a carpet. The weaver supplied a strong cotton string that composed the woof. The material in the balls did not need to be new, or even very strong.

The weaver had a system. He told us how many pounds of rag balls were needed to make a square yard. If we wanted a certain number of yards and lacked a few balls, he would sell us the number of balls we needed. If we had more than was required, he would buy the surplus.

That floor covering was quite useful. Floors were made of rough-sawed boards and needed covering to protect bare feet.

Making the balls was a family task. On rainy days out would come the rag bag. We children would sit on the floor, cutting the scrap material into strips. The older children helped with the sewing.

It did me no harm. Throughout my life I have been able to sew on my own buttons, if necessary.

About Pocket Watches

*T*he man who carries a stem wound pocket watch today is somewhat old fashioned, but time was when such a man was regarded with admiration by his fellows. His watch was a status symbol.

I know this from observation. My father was a farmer, but he had a set of nimble fingers and a good eye.

So he was the neighborhood watch repairman. He had a few small screwdrivers. He made a fine brush to clean parts, and he made his own oil. I think, but am not sure, that he made it from marrow taken from the leg bone of a deer.

The watches he repaired, free of charge, mostly were wound with keys. They were huge timepieces, compared with today's watch. Thus the gears and pinions were large enough to be managed without use of a watchmaker's eyepiece. I believe three of those watches would have weighed a pound.

The cases were sturdy, usually silver or nickel-plated, with lids that flipped open at the pressing of a switch. That exposed the face and the hands that were protected by a fragile crystal.

Sometimes the watch cases were gold plated, but those were carried chiefly by office workers.

The gold watch usually was carried in a vest pocket. It was fixed firmly to the end of a chain worn draped across the owner's chest. The chain itself was a prideful possession.

I remember one made of gold nuggets found in Alaska by its owner.

I recall several that were woven from hair taken from the tails of horses. Partly black, partly white, they were quite ornamental.

19

About Pocket Watches

Another I recall distinctly was braided from the hair of the owner's wife who had let him clip enough for the ornament.

The keys needed to wind those watches often were worn on the chains, a handy arrangement for the daily winding.

The last key-wound watch I remember seeing was one I bought from a country con-man after I had left home to work on a farm.

He first convinced me that I should have a timepiece, then persuaded me he had just the watch for me. It wasn't running, but any watchmaker could fix it, I was assured.

So I gave him $7, my pay for seven days of work, and proudly walked into town.

There a repairman bid $7 to make it run, an offer that convinced me I had been taken. Ever since that day I have been shy of men with key-wind watches for sale.

Six Syllables Savored

In the days of my childhood our family lived in a one and two-syllable community. We used short words. A farmer would plow his field, plant his wheat, oats or barley. At harvest time he cut his grain.

We had a few farmers who on occasion became intoxicated, but we never used that word. They got drunk, which was nothing to gossip about. The farmer who broke an arm or a leg used short words to describe his misfortune, though he didn't call it that. It was simply bad luck.

We weren't concerned with such things as transitive and intransitives. A farmer learned his son how to shoe a horse or hone a knife.

Our illnesses were simply catalogued. The person who became tubercular had lung trouble.

Geese in flight did not migrate, they flew.

It seems remarkable that we did so well in communicating. Mostly we used one syllable words, though we did not shun those of two syllables. But three syllables? Almost never, and then only at the risk of being called educated fools, or worse.

For me that situation changed when I was 11. That summer the community was holding Sunday school classes in our one-room school. John Osterhout, one of my friends, invited me to go home with him. His mother was cooking a kettle of stewed hen with dumplings, a dish always hard for me to ignore.

John had come riding one of the Osterhout farm horses; I was afoot. He admitted to me that he had been told not to let anyone ride behind him; the horse was sure to buck if that happened.

We decided it was safe to ride double, a decision that set me upon a course of vocabulary building.

The horse did buck, and we did fall off. The horse set out briskly for home, a mile away, and we followed in deep apprehension.

As we trudged soberly toward the crest of a hill, John's mother met us in motherly anger.

"Didn't I tell you not to ride that horse double? And didn't you promise? she scolded.

Before John could think of an answer she uttered the word that may have changed my life.

"Now don't contradict me," she said. "You know I won't stand being contradicted."

I never before had heard that three or four syllable word. I rolled it on my tongue like a morsel of tasty food. It seemed that, snowball like, it gathered other words, until I eventually had a sizable vocabulary.

The dinner, incidentally, was excellent, though John and I ate it in silence.

Doc Fann, Dentist

*I*n the mountainous country of Northern Idaho, Doc Fann had all the qualifications for an anomaly. Ours was a region that offered few ordinary comforts, and those who survived had to work hard.

Doc (we never called him doctor) was a dentist, reared and educated in one of the Virginias or Carolinas. Dentists were rare in the first decade of this century and I suppose he could and should have been busy in his profession. But he chose not to be.

Doc generally was regarded as averse to gainful work, though goodness knows he had reason to keep busy. He had six children.

Doc was a fastidious person, tall, straight as a Sitka spruce, keen of eye and bearded. He seldom worked on his homestead, depending on his gun to provide venison for his family. He had a knack of finding deer when his neighbors were unable to see even a hoof-print.

Once a year, in mid-summer, he became an itinerant dentist. As far as I knew, he never worked on any of his neighbors, but found his patients in nearby communities.

He hauled his equipment in a light rig (we called it a hack) pulled by two horses. I suppose the largest tool he had was his "engine" or drilling device for cleaning out cavities. It was foot-powered. When he worked on a patient he spread his chisels, picks and pliers on a folding table.

With these simple tools he went from door to door in town and country, often trading his services for cured hams, bacon, beans, flour, apples or other foods.

He was partial to patients who would pay at

least a part of his bill in cash.

When he ended his tour, usually late in the fall, he had his hack filled with food and a wallet full of money with which to buy clothing for his family.

That virtually ended his year's work.

Doc finally proved up on his homestead, sold it and moved away. In doing that he abandoned a chance to make a fortune, as fortunes were measured in those days.

The man who bought the Fann homestead had a couple of ambitious sons. Within a short time they cleared a little field which they planted to clover. They became seed farmers, producing a crop in one year that yielded $10,000 cash.

What they realized, but Doc Fann didn't, was that their virgin land was completely weed-free. The first year's crop was worth about four times what their father had paid for the 160-acre homestead.

Kip Kip's Ferry

*I*t never occurred to me in the years I knew Kip Kip to ask him how and where he got his odd name. Indians formerly were named for some personal deed or experience like Broken Jaw or Crazy Horse. But when missionaries came they often christened neophytes with names like Joseph and David.

There may have been some precedent for giving the Northwest Indians double names. We lived in an area that did have names that repeat, names like Lolo, an Idaho river, or Walla Walla, a Washington city.

Kip Kip was a member of the Nez Perce tribe. I believe he was about 50 years old, a stocky, deliberate man who had become an entrepreneur; he operated a ferry crossing the Clearwater River at Kamiah, Idaho.

His ferry was one of those propelled by the force of the river's current. By use of a series of pulleys running on a cable suspended over the water, Kip Kip could swing his craft around and the river would do the rest.

During the trip across he would forecast the weather for his patrons.

On reaching the shore he would use a long pole to beach the ferry, then drop an apron and the customers would drive off.

Kip Kip lived near his ferry landing. If he were not on duty, we would ring a bell and he would respond. For a two-horse rig he charged 25 cents. The customer with four horses and wagon paid 50 cents.

Sometimes when we were short of money, we would go on down the river a mile to the railroad bridge, tie our team or saddle horse, walk across and hike back to the town.

Kip Kip's Ferry

Finally progress came to Kamiah. A promoter got the idea of building a toll bridge. A subscription list circulated among homesteaders raised enough money to get the project started.

Kip Kip threatened to build another bridge and make it free. He said he had saved his money and had enough to do the job. But the promoter had his way.

The bridge builders made slow progress. First they drove a string of piling all the way across the Clearwater. Then they attached a shaky walkway and homesteaders used that for a time, which troubled Kip Kip because of the risk.

That winter a heavy flow of ice hit the piling and took it out, halting work for a time, but eventually the bridge was completed. It was a web-like steel structure that shook alarmingly every time a team pulled a wagon across.

Eventually the state assumed responsibility, replacing the toll structure with a free bridge built of reinforced concrete.

That bridge is performing well, but one thing it does not do — it does not give patrons the benefit of an Indian's weather forecasts.

The Grindstone

*I*t is not without reason that the grindstone is written into our metaphors as a harsh symbol of tedious toil. Most of us at one time or another have voiced the belief that we had our noses to the grinding wheel that once kept tools sharp.

Years have passed since I saw or used one of those instruments of torture; new devices and new methods have taken its place, but I shall never forget the one I knew in my youth.

Our mountain farm had no grindstone, but we had axes, scythes, sickles, chisels and knives to sharpen, and a neighbor had a grindstone we were welcome to use.

The grindstone we used was a disc of fine gray sandstone perhaps 18 inches in diameter and three inches thick. A square hole through the center of the disc had been fitted with a shaft or axle to which a crank had been attached. The axle was mounted crosswise on a frame made of 2x4 lumber which was supported by four legs.

My task was to apply boy power to the crank while my father pressed a tool against the turning stone. We mounted a quart tin can above the wheel and punched a hole in the can so that a trickle of water fell upon the grinding surface to keep it clean and cool.

It took a degree of skill and a steady hand to hold the dull tools at the correct angle, and my father was good at that. A mowing machine sickle containing about 40 cutting edges was the most delicate tool we had to sharpen.

Sharpening an ax was simpler, but it was to be dreaded because it took longer. The cutting edge had to be ground to a nickless line of steel. Then the thicker part of the blade had to be worn away. A thin ax blade was desired by the woodsman. That required hours of work.

Knives were treated with gentle care. Father would grind a while, then test the edge of the blade with his callused thumb. Later he honed the knives on a fine oil stone.

My chief memory of the periodic operation is of the blisters worn on my hand by the crank handle.

I had one consolation. Sometimes father drafted one of my brothers to turn the grindstone while I cut wood, hoed weeds in the garden or did some other non-blistering task.

From those days onward "keeping my nose to the grindstone" was more than just an idle phrase.

West's Settlers Tough

A merican pioneers, those doughty men and women who conquered the prairies and mountains of the West, were made of stern, unyielding stuff.

Such a man was my father. Born in Indiana in 1860, he stood six-feet-one in his stockings. What he lacked in book learning he compensated for in brawn.

He had spent his childhood in the swamps of Indiana. (They aren't there any more.) He was given calomel, a common remedy for the ever-present malaria. As a result, he used to tell us, his teeth were salivated, a term I never quite understood.

Later in life he had terrible toothaches, even in teeth that obviously were sound. Finally, after he had settled his family in Idaho, he decided to have his teeth removed.

The only dentist available for major extractions had an office a day's travel by wagon from our isolated homestead.

In December, the fall work was done; Father thought he could spare a few days.

Our only marketable product was fence posts cut from the farm's stand of timber. Dad loaded 150 on his wagon and took them to trade with a prairie farmer 20 miles away. The posts would bring him a few sacks of barley and oats that would help pay the dentist. Next day he would get his teeth removed early; then he would start home.

Dentistry in those days was done without cocaine. His teeth came out reluctantly and it was mid-afternoon before he hitched up his four horses and started for home.

By that time snow had begun falling. It quickly gained blizzard strength, whirling across the prairie in a mad attack on man and beast.

After four miles on the lonely road, he was so sick in body and spirit that he decided to seek refuge with a farmer he did not know.

Struggling to the farmhouse door, he explained his plight through swollen gums to the woman who answered his knock.

Her reply was, "We don't run a hospital or livery stable," and she closed the door.

It was nearly five miles to the next farmhouse. He knew he and his team had to find shelter. Fortunately that farmhouse was occupied by a man more merciful than the woman had been.

Not only did he have empty stalls and feed for the horses, but he let Dad make his bed in a manger, protecting him from the bitter wind.

Next day Dad drove on home, about 10 miles across the Clearwater River canyon.

As a reward for such fortitude, he deserved better than he received. His dentist tried twice, but never was able to fit him with wearable dentures. He spent the next 33 years with no teeth, but he never complained.

Complaints were not characteristic of the breed.

Early Day Remedies

The modern physician doubtless will smile or frown at methods used 60 years ago to treat human ailments. But people in those days did the best they could.

There were no doctors within easy reach of our early home in the Bitterroot Mountains of Idaho.

Thus we relied upon remedies, or presumed remedies, that had been used by grandmother and perhaps by her grandmother — the mother-to-daughter solutions we could draw upon in time of emergency.

For croup we used a half teaspoon of honey dissolved on the tongue. The remedy helped clear irritated throats, and it still does. A teaspoon of honey was used, too, as an effective cure for hiccups.

Many a time we cooked flaxseed and made a poultice to spread upon an afflicted part of the body. I do not know whether it cured anything. Never do I hear of it being used today.

Another poultice that was popular, and especially for treatment of boils, was made of bread and milk. It was credited with "drawing" the boil to a head. Then it could be lanced with father's all-purpose pocket knife.

At the first opportunity in spring we had a big mess of dandelion greens. Besides being good as a change of diet, they were supposed to be good for us. We had a notion that the greens supplied a generous amount of iron for our systems.

One of the popular nostrums of the time was the asafetida bag, which a child was supposed to wear suspended on a string looped around his neck. It was thought to be a bulwark against disease. It certainly was an anti-social nostrum. The odor of the stuff was something to remember.

From my father's frontier remedies came the idea of a lodestone that was supposed to develop in the stomach of a deer. It had magical powers to keep disease away, if only one could be found. Neither father nor I ever got one.

Treatment for broken bones called for no hocus pocus remedies. The patient was splinted and wrapped the best that we could manage and put to bed. The treatment may not have produced a straight limb, but it had to do.

Of all the remedies we used, I can recall only two that have withstood the test of medical developments.

Quinine and castor oil were the bane of every child I knew. Both have their place in the modern physician's bag, although each now is prepared in a manner to lessen the probability of childhood protest. (April 26, 1967)

Mailman on Horseback

When my postman fails to make a "swift completion of his appointed rounds," which sometimes happens, I remember Martin Andersen.

Martin was a tall, shallow-chested Dane who carried the mail on a Star Route that served the Northern Idaho area where the McCrackens were homesteaders.

He delivered mail to about 24 families along the 7 miles of his route, making the trip on horseback.

The mail was carried in weather-resistant bags, one for each patron. Martin made the route on Tuesdays and Fridays, no matter what the weather.

For his services he received $25 a month, and was considered a fortunate man. His job was awarded on bids.

Today it seems that his pay was small, but it was surprising how much food and clothing it would buy then.

Martin kept two horses for his work. He hung the patrons' mail bags on the saddle horn.

The Anderson homestead was about 1 1/2 miles along the route from our place. If the weather was bad, maybe hot or maybe cold enough to make the road icy, Martin would stop and change horses on the way in. He always carried a raincoat behind the saddle.

After reaching the town of Kamiah, he would sort the mail that awaited delivery, putting it in the proper sacks. These sacks were placed in rotation, so that when he reached a stop, the right bag would be handy. He would hang the bag on a designated post or tree, from which the patron would retrieve it.

Mailman On Horseback

While in town Martin took care of any business we might have with the Post Office. He would buy stamps for us. If we needed a postal money order, he brought it to us.

The mail we received was very important -- to us, anyway.

We seldom received letters, but regularly there was the Twice-A-Week Spokeman Review, the Youth's Companion and the Scientific American.

As far as I know, Martin never hurried his horse beyond a walk. Thus it took him all day to ride the route. And I do not recall that he ever was unable to make a "swift completion of his appointed rounds."

Electrical Storm

*T*he sun that sultry August evening went to rest in a fiery bed carved from the lip of the sky. The afternoon had been hot and oppressively still. I was 13 and longed for a dip in any pond that was deep enough for a swim.

But there was no swimming for me. We were busy with the harvest on a Northern Idaho prairie. My father was the threshing machine engineer; I was along more or less for the ride.

That afternoon the atmosphere seemed to be filled with something that gave me a sense of uneasiness. The hour of dusk was brief and the farmer for whom we were threshing surveyed the darkening sky with foreboding. He and my father were friends.

"Looks bad to me, John," he said. "Lightning is showing in the west."

At first I could see nothing unusual. Then I noted a distant intermittent glow. It was too far for me to hear thunder.

The farmer invited us to make our bed in his barn to escape the possibility of rain, and we accepted. Normally we spread our blankets under the open sky.

Before night had swallowed the last of the day we were ready to rest under a roof. By that time I could hear the distant roll of thunder, each resounding clap registering a little louder than its predecessor, though it was long seconds after the lightning before the sound reached me.

I went to bed, but not to sleep. Father and the farmer stood talking in the doorway. I heard father telling of a barn he had seen destroyed by lightning in Nebraska; the stock in the barn had been killed.

Electrical Storm

It was the better part of an hour before the storm reached us. Now the lightning flash and the thunder were almost simultaneous. There was no rain and none came from the clouds over us. Just the sound and fury of an electrical storm.

Alone in my bed, it seemed that my world surely was coming to an end. Never in my life had I felt so hopelessly helpless.

The barn groaned as if in misery. The four horses tied to the manger reared and screamed in fright as they tried to break free of their halters. It was the only time I ever heard a horse scream, a terrifying sound.

I dug deeper into my bed and wondered how my father and his friend could be so callous in such danger.

After what seemed an eternity, the interval between the flashes and the thunder became longer, indicating the storm had drifted away. Worn by my fears, I soon was asleep.

During my life I may have been nearer to death, but on no other occasion has the danger appeared more real or menacing.

When Trees Grew Hay

I suspect that one of the strangest fodders ever fed to cattle is a moss that grows on pine trees in Northern Idaho.

It's the moss of a greenish gray parasite that clings to the limbs of small pines — trees not more than 12 inches in diameter at the ground.

The first use we found for the moss growing on our homestead was for packing fragile things being prepared for mailing. My father wanted to send his prized stem-wound watch to a Chicago watchmaker. The moss was light and slightly springy and thus made excellent packing.

This moss is slightly sweet and I believe a rare sugar could have been refined from it, but the idea never occurred to us. It also contained a small amount of turpentine drawn from the trees.

It grew in clumps that sometimes gained a length of 15 inches. In winter the snow often accumulated on these clumps, causing them to pull away from their fragile mooring and fall to the ground.

The trees on which the moss grew usually stood fairly close together. As the winter snow began melting it left bare ground around each tree. The cattle knew this and would wallow through the snow to pick up the fallen food.

That gave us an idea. There were years when we did not have enough hay to feed our stock through the winter. As spring approached, we had to ration hay carefully, a practice that did not appeal to the cattle. Cows would moo plaintively in their hunger.

There was no hay to be purchased, even if we had the money to buy it.

It was then we began cutting the pines. As the trees fell, our cattle would rush eagerly into the limbs for the food-rich moss.

That was a device of last resort. We feared the loss of our small herd if fodder was not found to carry it for a week or two until the snow was gone. Then the cattle would feed on bunch grass on canyon slopes nearby.

I don't remember that we ever salvaged those pines that were sacrificed to save the herd. They weren't big enough for saw logs, and usually were not accessible as a source of firewood.

Had they not been cut for the moss, they eventually would have grown large enough to send to a mill.

All this happened before people understood there is a limit to what Nature will produce.

Grandfather's Role

*T*he role of a grandfather has undergone some changes during my lifetime. In the years when I was growing up "Gramp" was a man to reckon with.

Traditionally he was a storehouse of wisdom, an oracle to rely upon. He knew things from experience that the younger generations could not even guess.

Gramp could make a willow whistle, a bow and arrow, and hone a fine edge on a pocket knife. He knew the right time to sow wheat, to plant potatoes and to go fishing. This knowledge came from observing the moon and the stars, he said.

The autumn of each year was a time for him to come into his glory, for this was the period for making sauerkraut and for curing the coming winter's supply of hams and bacon. These were his special fields.

The kraut was put down in a stone crock, a five-gallon container into which we placed the finely cut cabbage, a little at a time. Between each addition of cabbage we tamped the cuttings with a piece of maple tree formed into a mallet. When juice began to rise over the cabbage it was time for more cabbage.

Each layer of cabbage received a generous sprinkling of salt. When the container was nearly full we placed a maple board on top of the cabbage, weighted it down with a well-washed stone from the river and set it away in a dark place for a month or six weeks.

The family cured hams and sides of bacon at about the same time. The fresh meat was cut to the desired sizes, trimmed and drained before the expert was called in. The pieces were laid out on a work bench with the rind sides down.

Gramp came now with an air of mystery and mastery. He spread over the meat a mixture of salt-peter, brown sugar, a sprinkling of black pepper, and a little vinegar. A few days later he applied another coating of the mixture, then left it to "cure" in a dark room for a couple of weeks.

From here on there was no call for special skills. The bacon and ham were hung in a smoke-house into which an improvised stove poured smoke from maple wood.

Each day we built a fire to make smoke until the meat had taken on a deep brown coloring. It gave off an unforgettable aroma; then it would keep for months. When sliced and fried it gave off an aromatic testimony to Gramp's skill.

There may be a grandfather who can perform those miracles today. I won't rule out the possibility, but I don't know of one. Nor do I know of a modern meat market that sells ham and bacon equal to that of my boyhood. In fact, I have a notion they just don't make ham, bacon, sauerkraut — or grandfathers — like that any more. (Sept. 26, 1965)

Indian Pole Roads

*T*he Indians I knew as a boy were a dispirited remnant of a once proud and self-sufficient tribe that occupied part of Idaho, Washington and Oregon. In their tribal prime they had a system of "highways" that puzzled me for years, although now I think I understand.

Evidence of that system was a series of parallel furrows that crossed our Idaho homestead. None of the furrows was more than 10 inches deep. About a dozen in number, they led through the forest to the eastward, or away from the Clearwater River Canyon.

The same type of furrows crossed the Nez Perce Prairie, although by the time I observed them they were becoming obliterated. Farmers were plowing them out of existence.

While we always understood those furrows had been made by Indians, it has been only recently that I discovered their significance. Now I find they were evidence of seasonal migrations that enabled the tribe to find food and a way of life.

These gentle people moved about in groups, taking with them all they owned. They moved with the seasons.

In winter they pitched camp along the rivers, in deep canyons where temperatures were milder. There the large herds of horses they used could find grass. In summer the natives broke camp and followed the deer and other game into the high country.

They found fruits and herbs in the mountains in summer. A few miles east of our homestead there was a large meadow where starchy camas roots, or onions, could be dug in quantity. The women accu-

41

mulated great sacks of camas to be ground and mixed with berries. Deer were killed and converted to jerky for winter use.

Those migrants had no wheeled vehicles. Instead, they devised a "vehicle" made of two long poles, each lashed to a surcingle, or belt, around the horse's belly. These poles formed a travois that was dragged behind the horse. They served as a truck and even the ambulance when one was needed. Indians took their sick and injured with them.

It was the dragging of the poles that marked the Indian routes. It was customary for the tribe to migrate to the Columbia and the Snake rivers for the salmon runs. Some of their young men crossed the Rockies to kill buffalo in Montana and I suppose they cut trails across that state with their travois.

Now these marks of an ancient culture have all but vanished. (Dec. 14, 1970)

People & Places

Baja Trail Blazer

Not many people know who Howard Gates was. (He has passed on now.) So I'd better introduce him.

He was a big man, strong of arm and sturdy of back. He was one of those men who didn't know his own strength. I think he was a botanist. At least, he made his living with flowers and plants.

One part of his commercial activity was the propagation and sale of cactus, for which he had an affinity. With Anaheim as his base, he had searched California's deserts for unusual specimens and for stock to be sold.

I believe it was 1929 or perhaps a year later that he undertook a phenomenal adventure.

Howard bought a one-ton Ford Model A truck (they don't make 'em like that anymore!) He equipped it with the best heavy-duty tires available, and built an enclosed sheet-metal body on the chassis.

Inside the truck he stored a 50-gallon drum of gasoline and another of water. Also he took all the tools needed to repair his vehicle. He had a couple of guns, a camera and a portable typewriter. There were shovels, a pick and an ax in his equipment box. Also he carried a considerable amount of canned food to augment the wild game he killed along the way.

Thus equipped, he drove from the border to La Paz, almost at the southern tip of Baja California. Of course, he had permits for the trip and to dig and carry away plants. His only companion was a flop-eared dog.

Howard's daily diary of the trip read like an endurance contest with all the evil forces of an untamed country that fought against intruders. There were no roads, period. It is true that a couple of cars were reported to have made the trip, but Howard found no traces of other motoring adventurers.

There were days when he didn't move a wheel. The trackless mountains he crossed and re-crossed had to be conquered with pick and shovel and brawn. Occasionally he met natives and fortunately he spoke Spanish fluently. A few times he found Mexican ranchers who helped him with teams of horses or mules.

It took six weeks to reach the short stretch of oiled road serving farmers north of La Paz. Resting there, he was a curiosity, if not a hero, in the peaceful, isolated community.

A man of lesser mettle would have shipped the truck home, but not Howard. Replenishing his supplies, he retraced his route, returning in about four weeks of driving. He came back with his truck loaded inside and out with exotic cacti.

Howard Gates was a trail blazer. Other motorists have been driving to La Paz since, and each of them should contribute a mite for a monument commemorating Howard Gates.

A Woman to Remember

Not many Californians will remember Ginger Lamb, but that is not because she is easily forgotten. Take it from me, Ginger was a woman to remember, as her husband Dan was a man to remember.

Back in the Depression days, this couple, then young and filled with the zest for adventure, set out on a three-year trip that turned out to be one of the most gripping epics of land and sea that I ever have read.

Living in Orange County, they designed and constructed a sea-going canoe which they sailed and paddled down the coast and through the Panama Canal. They lived off the land and sea as they went. As with most people of that time, they had virtually no money.

Dan and Ginger began a trial run near Laguna Beach and made their first real landfall at San Diego. At that moment prospects for continuing the voyage were dim. They had overloaded their canoe, thinking they must take equipment and food that later proved unneeded.

In October, 1933, they cast off, fixing a course for the Coronado Islands about 10 miles southward. There they had to make a decision — should they turn back, or should they abandon much of their cargo? They chose the latter. Next day the canoe rode better.

For clothing they kept only the most essential garments. Both were powerful swimmers, a fact that saved their lives many times, and especially off the Mexican coast where they ran into a chubasco. For endless hours they fought merciless wind and churning seas to stay alive. They were in the sea more than in the canoe as they were driven farther and farther from shore.

A Woman to Remember

They survived more dead than alive. When the wind subsided they crawled into the canoe, sleeping until strength returned.

Weeks later they made camp in a protected cove, ate supper, spread their blankets and fell asleep on the beach. During the night a coyote attacked Dan, ripping the flesh on his hands to shreds. Dan killed the coyote but was faced with the problem of how to treat his wounds.

Ginger, fearing rabies, decided their only choice was to try to disinfect and cauterize the bites. She filled their largest cooking pot with water, added iodine and permanganate of potash crystals, and put it on their campfire.

Then she forced Dan to immerse his hands until the water boiled and he could no longer stand the pain. Rough treatment, but it worked!

Hunting treasure on desolate Cocos Island near the end of their voyage, they came near disaster when Dan was stricken with appendicitis. Ginger was terrified, yet reluctantly ready to perform surgery when an American tuna clipper hove to offshore.

The crew came ashore for a fresh-water bath but instead packed Dan in ice and headed for Costa Rica to seek life-saving medical help.

Eventually arriving in Panama, Dan, Ginger and their "Vagabunda" became the smallest craft and crew to transit the Canal — a record that stood for many years.

Why bring this up now? Because Ginger's quest for adventure is over. She passed away at the couple's home recently, having enriched adventure lore with one of its finest stories. (March 7, 1967)

Opportunity Backfires

*E*d Hicks was a tall, likable competitor of mine in a wildcat taxi business in Kellogg, Idaho. He was from Arkansas, sometimes called the Opportunity State. I thought I knew him well. I was wrong. I would have been nearer the mark had I taken him at his word.

As we waited at the curb for a chance fare one day, Ed told how he proposed to get rich. He would steal money, hide it, confess his crime, take a prison sentence and live happily forever on the stolen money. It would be his after he was free, he boasted. It was a slick scheme and he laughed easily as he told it.

Well, it happened soon after I left Kellogg in 1912. There was but one daily train through Kellogg eastward to Wallace. A Spokane bank had sent a packet of $12,000 (a large sum in those days) to a Kellogg Bank. No messenger was present to accept the package and it was left unguarded on the depot platform. Ed Hicks was there; no one else. Ed grabbed the package and made his get-away.

Bank and railroad detectives converged on the little city. For the most part they just listened. They found that Ed often met the train. They interviewed him and he readily admitted he had taken the money.

Ed Hicks was so open about it the officers could not believe him. Eventually he convinced them that he was the thief. He was taken to court and sentenced to five years in federal prison.

Before long he began to suspect he had made a mistake. He summoned the officers, hoping to make a deal. He offered to return part of the money for his freedom. No deal.

Opportunity Backfires

He next offered to deliver all of the money in return for his liberty. Still no deal. Then he said he would give up the money if he could visit his family. The authorities accepted.

But when he got back to Kellogg, under escort, he said the money had disappeared. Someone had taken it, he claimed. So, back to prison he went.

Long before the prison sentence was completed he caved in, this time promising to hand over the money. He took officers to the hidden cash and they took him back to prison, a beaten man.

Poor Ed. He had mistaken temptation for opportunity.

On Retirement

*L*iving as I do in a community of retired people, (there are 11,000 of them in close proximity to me) I am amazed at how many ended their professional and business careers with an abrupt finality.

For years they lived for the day when they could clean out their desks and turn their responsibilities over to their successors.

It seems to me that people who change their life patterns abruptly in that manner are denying society something priceless. All their lives they were learning a skill, a basis for judgment, or a profession.

Not all, of course, shape their retirement lives in that manner.

Standing against the philosophy of idleness and a life devoted to rest was the late Mme. Ernestine Schumann-Heink. Several times in her later years she "retired," only to return to her beloved and worshiping public.

It was in the depths of the "Great Depression" that I heard her in an open-air concert. Anaheim, the little city where I lived, raised a small sum to bring her there for an evening of unforgettable music under the stars.

She had lost the vigor that once projected her personality across the footlights to her applauding audiences. Her thinning hair was almost snow white. The lines of her body betrayed her age. Her face, deeply lined, supported my guess that she was 75 years old.

But when she walked slowly, majestically, to the front of the low stage, her audience forgot her age. She seemed to float on air.

On Retirement

Then she sang, and how she sang. Her voice was the voice of a woman who now was nearly sung out, but it was vibrant in a way not possible at other times of her life.

Now, nearly 30 years later, I can recall but one song she sang. It was Brahm's "Lullaby," a selection that required no high notes. At times it seemed that her voice was hoarse. At the concert's end she was recalled to sing the "Lullaby" over and over.

Had I not heard her my life would have been poorer, less meaningful.

Then she did something I shall never forget.

I had a young woman working on my small newspaper staff. As the sounds of applause died and the audience drifted away, the great operatic star took my associate by the arm and the two walked slowly through the park to the singer's car. There they sat for an hour while the older woman talked of the meaning of life.

Madame Schumann-Heink had something to give, right down to the last, and she gave it freely. (March 30, 1967.)

A Noble Pie Berry

*U*nless the totally unexpected happens, one of the noblest of pie berries soon will be only a memory in Southern California, and it's a pity, too.

The berry to which I direct this paean of praise was named for one of its unrewarded developers, the late Rudy Boysen. I knew Rudy when he was Anaheim park superintendent. He told me the story of his berry.

Rudy spent his boyhood in Oregon where several kinds of berries, both wild and domesticated, are to be found. Any one of them may have been the "father" of the Boysen. Rudy and a young friend had read about hybridization of plants and they decided to try their hand.

They took pollen from the wild dewberry and sprinkled it onto the bloom of an Oregon evergreen, or maybe it was the other way around. They took pollen from the Loganberry, from the wild blackberry, and even from a strawberry plant.

Then they planted seeds from the cross-fertilized bush and from those seeds came the plant that was to be named the Boysenberry.

Berries from it were widely acclaimed and the boys had visions of making a little fortune from their haphazard experiment.

About that time Rudy and his friend were summoned for military duty in the First World War. Before leaving, the boys made a hand-shake agreement with a man who was to pay them $5,000 for the plant. Rudy never told me the man's name. Indeed, he seemed to bear no ill will over what happened.

When Rudy returned to the United States in

A Noble Pie Berry

1921 his berry had been widely distributed in some manner that yielded no profit for him. As a result the boys received nothing for their discovery, except that Rudy had the plant named for him.

For a number of years Orange County was the Boysenberry capital of the world, to steal a phrase. Walter Knott planted five rented acres with Boysens and from that humble start came the multi-million-dollar Knott's Berry Farm.

And from that development came my own berry vines that produced many a huge bowl of fresh berries for my table and for my friends. Also from my vines came the filling for some of the tastiest pies ever to come my way.

Now, alas, search as you may and you will find no commercial plantings of Boysenberries in Orange County. I found a few acres of Boysenberries near Riverside and during two summers I have obtained a couple of flats. If my bank deposit box was equipped for such service, I think I'd keep my frozen hoard there, for mine is a treasure beyond compare. (Oct. 15, 1968.)

Anaheim's Flood

I well remember Feb. 27, 1938, and the four following days. The period had been preceded with normal rainfall so that the soil was well saturated in and around Anaheim, where I lived and worked.

Then heavy rain began falling, not to let up for nearly five days.

At first there was no alarm. The Santa Ana River, a few miles eastward, had been well diked. An embankment wide enough to accommodate a truck roadway surely would protect the city. The river channel would carry a stream about eight feet deep and more than 300 feet wide. We felt fairly safe from the runoff developing in San Bernardino and Riverside counties.

I slept peacefully the night the rain stopped, awakening at 5:30 a.m. There was an ominous silence in my neighborhood — no sounds of moving vehicles or of people.

Listening attentively, I heard the sound of moving water.

The dike had broken, our house stood in a sea of water 18 inches deep.

Dressing quickly in rough clothing, I ate a hurried breakfast, took my newly acquired press camera and started for the office, snapping pictures as I waded. One of my shots was of two young men gleefully rowing a boat down a main street.

At the offices of the Anaheim Bulletin I found water had flooded the motor pit under our press. That meant it would be impossible to print a newspaper that day. Our telephones were silent, as were our United Press teletype machines.

Anaheim's Flood

Certain there would be no paper to edit that day, I continued in my photographer role, gathering news notes as I waded almost waist deep through town.

Later in the day I took my films to the Los Angeles Times, nearly 30 miles away, and left them. I believed I could not use them, but The Times could.

Bone tired, I returned to my office to find my publisher, Lotus Louden, wanting to print a flood edition. The Fullerton Tribune had offered to print our paper, if we assembled one.

Could I get out a paper?

That was almost 6 o'clock. I sent word to the other three members of my loyal staff that we would go to work at midnight, and then drove to Los Angeles to recover my pictures. Back at my desk, I wrote two editorials and was ready with assignments when my reporters came in.

We published a 12-page edition entirely of local stories and pictures.

Then I went home to sleep 14 hours.

Gagging on Garlic

*T*he late Sam White was an obstinate man who refused to concede defeat easily. By trade, he was a carpenter, but the Great Depression deprived him of work in his craft, so he set out to meet the challenge of how to live in another way.

He owned about two acres of land on the pastoral outskirts of Anaheim. Though a small plot, it was big enough to get him a summer's fruitless work.

Sam had read somewhere of a man who in the previous season had made a very nice profit from raising garlic. It seemed like a good idea.

Not that Sam especially liked garlic, but he thought he could do what another man had done. His land was good and he had plenty of water, so he went to work.

He hired a fellow with a tractor to plow and harrow his little field. The rest of the project was pure muscle work. From early morning to late evening, he was in the field, pushing a cultivator, hoeing and irrigating. There was seldom a weed to be found on his "farm."

And the garlic responded with vigor. It filled the air with it penetrating aroma, causing some of the neighbors to make disparaging remarks. But Sam only smiled.

By early fall the crop would be harvested and marketed. Next year, he decided, he would plant something less likely to offend.

Thus he lived in hope during the summer. Then he made a discovery. A lot of other people had read the article about the man who made a profit with garlic.

Gagging on Garlic

As he went from one wholesaler to another without getting an offer, he decided he had made a mistake. After all, there's just about so much you can do with garlic, and a little of the pungent stuff goes a long way.

About Thanksgiving time he had to concede defeat. His neighbors were still slightly hostile. He was tired from his summer's work and there was no market for his garlic.

So Sam took his shovel and dug a deep hole in his field. Without ritual, he buried his crop and hired the tractor again to plow and harrow.

But he didn't give up.

That winter he planted his land to Boysenberries. And the next summer there were some berries — not many, but enough to foretell future production.

The second year the plants produced loads of berries, but Sam didn't sell many because few people had money. He did harvest a great crop of friendship among his neighbors, for he was a generous person. What berries he could not sell he gave way, still smiling.

At least he didn't have to bury the crop.

1925: Clear Air

*I*n the late winter of 1925 the editors of a Los Angeles newspaper dreamed up an idea that sounds utterly ridiculous today. They wanted to induce more people of the nation to come to California to make their homes.

Many things had been tried by others, but there were few visible results. Advertising hadn't done the trick. There had been an abundance of magazine and newspaper articles telling how really great this region is.

However, people living in the East and Midwest, and especially those who had never been here, refused to believe or be persuaded.

So, those innovative editors dreamed up a contest. They offered cash prizes for letters written by their readers to friends and relatives living elsewhere. Those letters were to extol the weather, the orange groves, the beauties of the seashore and the mountains, and the wide-open spaces.

The top prize went to a man who wrote of the prevalence of linnets that flitted about his window in winter. He told of the sparkling clear air that let people see the distant peaks. His letter had the ring of sincerity and I often wonder whether it persuaded Uncle Bill or Aunt Henrietta to leave their home in snowy Maine or New Hampshire.

My entry, written to a brother-in-law, won only $25. I believe it drew 10th prize. I do know it did not cause my wife's brother to move forthwith to California.

And yet, the sum total effect of those letters must have been tremendous, judging from what is happening. The editors of that same newspaper now are deeply concerned with what they refer to as over-population. California is the most populous of the states, and it still is growing. It seems the editors may have turned the spigot on and they do not know how to turn it off.

In 1925 it seemed unthinkable that there ever could be too many people here. Not in the lifetime of those then residing here, anyway. No one thought of ecology in those days, and I seriously doubt one person in a thousand knew the meaning of the word. Certainly I didn't.

Things like poisoned rivers, polluted air, over-crowded highways (freeways hadn't been built), smog — such concepts would have been good for laughs. California simply was too big to permit anyone to think seriously that we could have too many people here, or that they would bring too many automobiles. (Oct. 21, 1970)

"Signs of Progress"

Californians who point pridefully to the growth and the greatness of their state might profit by flipping the hands of the clock back a few years with me, and then turning them forward for a few more years.

Looking backward, which is easiest, I see broad level fields where strawberries and tomatoes were grown by the truck load. Other fields produced asparagus, lima beans, sugar beets, celery, melons and goodness knows what.

All this gave a sense of security, of food for the table, of freedom from want. It was an orderly, peaceful scene that invited city folk to drive into the farming areas.

Now juggle the time mechanism to the present.

Highways appear where there once were only roads. These are broad freeways that cut through farms, chewing up acres and acres of fields. Never again will this land produce the essential ingredient of a strawberry shortcake.

But worse is to be found where farms and groves once were so lush.

Vast fields of fertile ground have been taken by the sub-divider. He has installed streets, sewers and water systems, and around these evidences of civilization he has built houses. Thousands of acres of California's best farm land have been removed from any possibility of food production.

Now for a look into the future, and this calls for a little prodding of the imagination.

Where will we raise our food a hundred years from now? We will have splendid freeways, no doubt. We will have homes for the people. But where will we go on a Sunday afternoon to see cattle grazing, lettuce growing and cantaloupes being harvested?

Not at a city's edge, that's for sure — unless our civilization moves fast. There is little time for doing what must be done, and I assume it won't be done.

But we well might begin legislation looking toward preservation of farms from the despoilers who march in the name of progress. These are the people who preach land use. They assume that land is most useful when it provides the most homes for the most people.

Isn't it possible that land is most useful when it is supplying food? Or feeding our eyes with spirit-mending pastoral beauty?

As I have witnessed the so-called march of progress across our finest farm land, I have been troubled. Not that I expect to run short of food, but I would like some assurance that my grandchildren will enjoy these symbols of abundance. (June 11, 1963)

Alcatraz

*L*et me say at the outset that I never have been on Alcatraz Island, but I missed it only about a mile. For a period of tortured days, perhaps two weeks, I lived in sight of the former prison rock and that was enough for me.

In May, 1918, I was deposited on Angel Island, which is situated north of Alcatraz. I had come from Northern Idaho where there still was a little of winter's snow, and I came dressed for Idaho's climate.

It was near evening when I arrived. With a few hundred other men who were destined to become soldiers, I had dinner. Then I was given two thin wool blankets and a folding canvas cot.

Blowing in through the Golden Gate, a bone-numbing wind brought moisture-laden air that soon rolled a cloud of fog over the bay. The fog came in each night, never permitting the temperature to become comfortable while I was there. Alcatraz must have received the same nightly "bath."

That night, protected by my woolen long-johns, I slept fitfully. Next morning my fellow sufferers and I were "processed" into the Army. As is the custom, we were deprived of our clothing, weighed, measured, and inspected for identifying scars.

All of my heavy Idaho underwear, my warm suit — every shred of clothing — was taken away. I was given thin cotton shorts and undershirts, a cotton shirt, khaki pants, shoes and a hat with a chin strap to keep it from blowing away.

By the second night on the island I was thoroughly fed up with Army life and was looking forward to my bunk. That was a mistake.

Alcatraz

Soon I found there was no warmth in Army blankets. I laid them on the cot so there were two layers under me and then I wrapped them across my body two layers thick. Still I shivered.

Finally I got up and found a stack of newspapers which I spread in a thin layer on the cot, then replaced the blankets. The paper kept some of the wind from getting at me from the underside of the cot, but toward morning I gave up.

A guard walking his beat near me had managed to find fuel for a fire, and I became his fireman. After that I did exercises to keep warm.

I cannot recall exactly how many days I remained on Angel Island, but it seemed a very long time.

Often I looked across the chill waters of San Francisco Bay to the rocky island I now know was Alcatraz.

I can remember only one pleasant thing about Angel Island. There were geranium hedges along the paths, the first such plants I had seen.

Even that memory does not soften my appraisal of Angel Island, nor does it make me envious of those Indians who took possession of Alcatraz. Let them have it!

(Editor's note: This column was published in The Union of Dec. 9, 1969, following an attempt by American Indians to take over abandoned Alcatraz Prison.)

A Long 10 Seconds

As the clock measures time, 10 seconds is not very long. It is one sixth of a minute, to be exact. In 10 seconds one normally draws a breath three or four times and exhales an equal number of times.

But in terms of the time it takes Fate to make up its mind, it can seem an eternity.

I'll never forget the time Fate changed its mind about the USS Grant, a great freighter used in World War I as a troop transport.

As ships go today, the Grant was something of a pygmy, having a displacement of only 18,000 tons. But at the time of this incident it was regarded as a really big ship.

My outfit boarded her in New York Harbor one early November day. There were 6,500 troops and perhaps 300 crewmen aboard when the Grant slipped out to sea, alone.

A convoy of slower vessels was being made up, but our ship had enough speed (we hoped) to evade the enemy subs that were claiming so many Allied ships.

Troops were bunked down in tiers three high on six decks. Climbing out from the bottom deck was too much of a strain for anything but chow, which was served twice daily.

Mess was served on a section of the third deck. Tables about 25 feet long stood against the ship's hull, extending inward toward the middle of the deck.

We stood while eating, our hobnailed trench boots providing precarious footing on the metal deck when the ship lurched violently, as it frequently did.

The bottom-most portion of our cargo was a

considerable tonnage of steel rails. Riding low, they were calculated to provide stability.

The voyage was uneventful until we reached the Bay of Biscay, renowned among seamen as the "graveyard of ships." There we ran into a storm that tossed us about like a helpless cork. Waves ran high, smashing a huge lifeboat riding in davits 60 feet above the Plimsoll's line.

I was at mess when it happened.

The Grant, buffeted by a huge wave, rolled heavily and the rails used for ballast shifted. The ship lay far over on its side, unable to recover.

I grabbed the edge of the table with both hands and might have remained upright had a man at my right stayed on his feet. He let loose and came thudding against me. Together we mowed down the line of men all the way to the bulkhead where we lay in a helpless tangle.

Later we learned that the Grant stood in that position 10 seconds while Fate was deciding what to do with her and some 6,800 men.

Then a wave hit the ship on the low side, rolling the hull back to vertical. The shifting steel rails moved to their correct position where crewmen hastily lashed them down.

Another wave on the wrong side would surely have tipped us over causing one of the great disasters of the war.

Years later I saw the Grant in San Diego Harbor. It had resumed its role as a freighter and had been renamed the Schofield.

Runaway Train

*I*n spite of Casey Jones and other heroes of the rails, I must go on record with the statement that riding a runaway train makes poor entertainment.

My conclusion was gained in France. Our regiment had entrained at Brest for an all-night ride deep into Brittany.

Rumor had it, correctly it turned out, that our destination was a little city named Malestroit. It wasn't on the rail line, but that made no difference. We'd ride as far as possible, then march the remaining distance.

The cars we rode were the familiar "8 horses or 40 men" variety, dubbed Forty & Eight by the soldiers of World War I.

They were boxcars of a type never duplicated in the United States. There was one door that slid open. Along the door side of the car was a step used by brakemen to pass from one car to another.

There was no air brake system such as has been common on American trains for many years. Instead there was a long lever which the brakeman pressed down to force the brake shoes against the wheels. It surely wasn't the best idea ever developed for stopping a train.

The 40 men assigned to our car sat on straw spread on the floor. The night was cold and we huddled in our trench coats. There was total darkness in the car, except when a soldier lighted a cigarette.

There were 19 cars in our train, which was pulled by a huffing little locomotive. Occasionally the engine's whistle shrilled into the darkness. When the train was climbing a grade it was all the engine could do to huff us over. At times we barely moved as we crested a grade.

We slept fitfully. There was little opportunity to relieve our cramped legs.

Shortly after midnight I sensed we were climbing a long grade. Then our car, and a dozen behind us, stopped. The sound of the engine's exhaust increased rapidly. The train had broken in two.

Our part of the train began gliding back down the grade, gaining speed by the minute. Then out of the darkness came the sound of a voice so imperious it must have been an officer shouting:

"Everybody off the train! Everyone get off, now!"

Disciplined to obey, we slid the door open to see the moonlit countryside gliding past. A few men from the cars behind us already were on the ground. Men from our car were leaping from the brakeman's step.

Someone yelled another order:

"Push down on the brake levers!"

At the bottom of the grade the cars slowed and stopped; then were re-coupled with the locomotive. Those of us who had leaped off had to walk a half mile to re-board.

After that there was an investigation to learn who had ordered us off the train. Someone knew, of course, but no one ever told.

Tough Sergeants

*I*n my brief career in the Army (France in 1918) I came to look upon sergeants as prime exemplars of unreasonable toughness, and it was some years later before I became aware that the impression was at least partly wrong.

It was the late Rudolph (Rudy) Boysen, co-developer of the Boysenberry, who led me to think more kindly of that breed of taskmaster.

Rudy had been a sergeant in the expeditionary force sent into eastern Russia near the close of World War I. The troops were assigned to the task of subduing the Bolsheviks.

It was in the dead of winter when the Americans began to realize their worst enemy was the weather.

They were ordered to go to Vladivostok to board ships for their return home.

At the time they were perhaps 200 miles south of Archangel.

While waiting for the train that was to take them several days ride to the coast, a sergeant saw a little girl huddled on the station platform. She was crying.

All about her was desolation.

A soldier who knew a few words of Russian talked with the child, who was about 7 years old.

Her parents had been killed. Her home had been burned. She had no food and no place to go.

"Let's take her with us," a sergeant suggested, and that is what the Americans did. It was fun caring for the little waif. And it was rewarding to see her respond with a smile. The men taught her a few words of English, which, Rudy admitted to me, were not the best words in the language.

Arriving at the port of embarkation, the men suddenly awoke to the fact that they had a problem. They could not take the child with them and they had no place to leave her.

Someone suggested the 14 or 15 sergeants, who were her self-appointed guardians, take the girl to a convent at the edge of the city. They all went together to see the mother superior.

When they made their mission clear the kindly administrator said flatly, "No." The convent was caring for all the orphans it could support.

But, said a spokesman for the sergeants, they would pay. They pledged that each of them would contribute $15 a month for the care of the girl until she was able to manage for herself.

Ah, that was different. Surely the convent could find room.

Greatly relieved, the sergeants bid their little charge good-bye, made their first payment and embarked for home.

It was well into the Great Depression when Boysen told me the story and showed me a letter he had received from the convent. The girl had been graduated from the convent school and was employed as a secretary by a firm in China.

The letter released the sergeants from their pledge.

Not one of them had missed a payment, even in the Depression years.

Are sergeants tough? I don't believe it. (Feb. 18, 1969.)

San Diego Blackout

On the night of Dec. 7, 1941, San Diego went into hiding, but did a poor job of it.

Not many San Diegans knew the extent of Pearl Harbor's damage in the Japanese attack, and those who knew weren't talking.

They gathered in little groups and tried to decide what to do about the city's safety. They feared the Japanese would bomb the city to destroy warplane production facilities and naval installations.

Early that fateful afternoon, most San Diegans had put their cars away. I had driven mine to work, parking it near the Union-Tribune offices on Third Avenue. My job required that I work from 1 to 9 p.m. When my work was done, I faced the challenge of driving about seven miles to my home in East San Diego.

That night I left the office to find all street lights had been turned off.

Someone, I presume it was the police, had summoned a crew of former servicemen to enforce the no-lights idea.

Downtown I found driving was fairly easy. The large buildings silhouetted against the starry sky helped me know where I was.

I drove eastward on Broadway, at about 15 miles an hour, until I came to 12th Avenue. I was afraid to make a left turn there, with the car lights out and the streets dark as printer's ink. So I flicked my lights on for a fraction of a second.

The intersection was clear and I drove through.

I suppose a Japanese submarine could have seen the light for 10 miles, but I observed other drivers were taking the same quick safety precaution.

Also by rolling the car windows down, I could hear approaching vehicles.

Park Boulevard, with few intersections, was less hazardous. I poked past the dim outline of Naval Hospital, using memory and starlit eucalyptus trunks to guide me through Balboa Park. Reaching El Cajon Boulevard, I met a guard who had a red-hooded flashlight. He waved me through and I crept eastward to 40th Street.

So I completed one of the most nerve-wracking drives I ever made.

Then, looking westward, I saw the sky was bright from the lights at Convair where night crews were assembling PBYs and B-24 bombers.

It was a blueprint of how not to try to hide a city.

Santa Ana Winds

*E*ach year at this time it is necessary, I believe, to explain what Santa Ana winds are and how they got their name.

Otherwise there are people who feel reluctant to call them by their proper name lest they affront residents of the city of Santa Ana. Also there are people in Santa Ana who feel they are being put upon by users of the term.

Those dry winds received their name from the fact that they seem to reach Orange County through Santa Ana Canyon, which is a delusion. Santa Ana Canyon was christened by Gen. Gaspar Portola, who probably was the first white man to traverse that gorge.

July 26, 1769, Portola came down through Santa Ana Canyon with a small party of soldiers and pitched camp on a river near where the town of Olive now stands. Since it was St. Anne's Day, he named the river after that saint, and the name later was changed to Santa Ana.

Long after that Santa Ana was founded on the alluvial plain below Portola's camp site.

Nobody thought about the winds at that time, except when they were blowing. That might be at any time between September and April. The winds could well have been called foehn winds; similar winds called foehns blow in the Alps. In Southeast Asia there are winds like the Santa Anas and they are called brickfelders.

Nearly 40 years ago Santa Ana residents became sensitive about these hot, grit-laden winds. They wanted to rid themselves and their city of any idea that they owned or created the disturbances.

So, through their Chamber of Commerce they asked the news media to call the winds "desert winds."

It didn't take, probably because they really aren't desert winds.

Then they suggested the winds be called "santanas" after what they said was an Indian word meaning devil winds. Students of Indian languages exploded that idea; there never was such a word in the Indian tongues, they said.

Then it was suggested they be called Santa Annas after the Mexican general of that name. The general was said to have chased cattle across the American deserts, stirring up clouds of dust.

That one failed, too. The name of the general is not spelled the same as is the name of the winds. Moreover, the name of the winds was fixed before the general was born, and besides, he never was in the area where the winds blow.

Santa Anas are generated in a high pressure area over Utah and Arizona, flowing toward a low pressure pool over the Pacific Ocean. As the winds approach the coast, they drop off the highlands onto the coastal plain. For each 1,000 feet of elevation they lose, they gain 5 degrees of temperature. Thus, by the time they reach sea level they are miserably dry and hot. (Dec. 15, 1969)

Power to Destroy

*T*he oft-repeated statement that taxes have the power to destroy has been proved anew in Orange County.

A little more than 35 years ago Mrs. Susanna Bixby Bryant, widowed daughter of a pioneer family that once owned vast tracts of land in Los Angeles and Orange counties, conceived of a splendid project that would honor California's pioneers. It was to be a useful undertaking, and perhaps one that no other public benefactor would have thought of.

Mrs. Bryant was heir to Rancho Santa Ana, a large acreage situated in Santa Ana Canyon, east of the city of Anaheim. While much of the property was too hilly for agriculture, a considerable area was in the canyon floor. This level land was planted to citrus; the hilly area was used for grazing.

The grand idea was to develop a botanical garden in which every plant native to California would be grown.

She dedicated nearly 100 acres for the venture, and endowed it with what she thought would be ample funds for its perpetuation. A brilliant young botanist was hired to search the mountains and the deserts for plants and seeds.

A crew of workers skilled in making and laying adobe brick erected the great house that was to serve as headquarters.

Most of the construction was done during the depression when wages were not high, and still the building cost Mrs. Bryant $110,000.

A foundation with a board of directors was created. Tax exemption was provided because it was a semi-public educational institution, a place where botany students could find native specimens without excessive search and travel.

Not long after seeing the project completed, Mrs. Bryant died. It was thought advisable, by the foundation directors, to move the garden to a site nearer a major educational institution. The plants so studiously gathered were taken to a location near Pomona, and the garden property was restored to the tax rolls.

No one wanted to pay the annual levy against the fine adobe house; hence it was torn down — destroyed.

This was not precisely the sort of action foreseen by Britain's Lord Acton when he made his observation about the destructive power of taxes, although it seems to prove a point. It was a $110,000 point. (Jan. 4, 1965)

Before Zippers

I met Fritz, fine tailor for men, perhaps 10 years B.Z. (before zippers), and our meeting caused him regrettable embarrassment.

Fritz (he had a surname, but I like a tone of familiarity) owned a fine store for men. Nothing but the best was stocked, but the owner rarely was behind the counter. He hired clerks for that and spent his time in the tailor shop at the rear of the store.

The lower floor of the shop was ringed with shelves stacked with bolts of woolen cloth from the mills of Scotland and England. A customer wanting to order a suit dealt with Fritz.

Proudly the tailor brought his imported weaves, unrolled enough to display the pattern, wrapping it around his thigh to simulate a trouser leg, or draped it over the customer's shoulder.

Fritz had a standard of workmanship an employee might not be able to achieve. His suits didn't need a label. People in the town just knew it had come from his shop. That limited the number of suits he could sell, but that was all right with Fritz.

The day I first met him he was on the balcony above his display room. He was sitting on top of his cutting table, busily sewing by hand.

Sitting there, his knees drawn up and his shins crossed, he was so busy he didn't notice me until I spoke. When he looked up he flushed, slightly angry and embarrassed.

Later I learned why. Fritz had his training as an apprentice in Germany. There he had been taught that tailoring was the lowest form of work a man could do. After his apprenticeship he had migrated to the United States and then on to Anaheim, the little German-speaking community where I found him.

His skill with his needle and shears, plus his energy and willingness to do humble tasks, had brought him money. His investments had enabled him to buy his store, a number of business buildings, an orange grove, a nice home and a substantial interest in a savings and loan association.

He was a man highly respected in his community, and yet he felt that his calling was demeaning.

He was making buttonholes on a pair of trousers when I met him.

"This is silly work," he muttered. "It needn't be done this way."

"How else could it be done?" I asked, puzzled. "Trousers must have buttons and buttons must have holes."

"No, you are wrong," the tailor said positively. "I invented a thing called a zipper to replace buttons. It was very good and I had a barrel of them made. But no one wanted zippers. They are down in the basement now."

This tailor, who made the finest button holes I've ever seen, was 10 years ahead of his time with the zipper idea.

No, he didn't patent his invention. Someone else came along and did that.

Crash Kills Dream

*I*t's a little strange that I should remember his name after 40 years. Freddie Thaikol was a human meteor flashing along the perimeter of my life, then was gone.

Freddie was a small man of 30. His blue eyes burned with the glow of self-confidence. He knew what he knew and he had the ability to fire others with his zest, even though his Austrian-learned high school English seemed at times to fail him.

I think Freddie clings to me in memory because he had been a part of a world tragedy before I met him, and was to become a part of his own tragedy.

He came out of World War I and somehow found his way to the little Orange County town of Brea.

He was alone, and yet he was not alone, for he was ridden by an idea that always was with him.

With no apparent great effort he persuaded a few Brea men to back him in building what he announced would be the world's smallest practical airplane.

His backers obtained an unused warehouse for his shop. He set up a drawing board and put his plans on paper. The plane was to be a one-man craft. If the design had defects they were not noted by the eager group that gathered around as he pieced the framework together. As I recall, he covered the frame with canvas.

It didn't take Freddie long to assemble the plane. He bought a little motor and a propeller. When completed the plane was so light that two strong men could have carried it away. By modern standards it was odd.

Because the plane was hardly thicker than a man's body, the pilot had to lie on his stomach.

The first test flight was not widely advertised. It took place over an open field and was pronounced a great success, although the plane soared barely 600 feet off the ground.

Freddie and his backers were thrilled, as was the volunteer pilot.

The next flight was different. Several hundred Breans had gathered for the event.

The little plane zoomed skyward, and the enthusiasm of the spectators soared with it. Again it reached 600 feet.

Then it happened. For no reason ever determined the plane disintegrated, falling into the field.

Everyone ran to the wreck — everyone but Freddie. The pilot was killed; Freddie vanished without a trace.

Four days later he walked into the police station, haggard and drawn.

"Hello, we've been looking for you," the officer at the desk said.

"I know, I've come back to be arrested," said Freddie.

"Arrested?"

"Yes. In my country I would be held as a criminal for building a plane that failed."

He wasn't arrested, of course. But Freddie Thaikol left Brea and now he is only a speck in memory. (Oct. 4, 1968)

Going, Going, Gone

With the passing of years the importance of lost history has been impressed upon me. Not the big events of history — they can be found recorded in treaties, in declarations by heads of state, in current newspaper microfilms.

The history I bemoan consists of the little things that deeply concerned communities and individuals in days gone by.

Recently I wanted to learn the history of a place once widely known as Anaheim Landing. No longer is it so known, and before many years have passed it will not even live in tradition — the father-to-son tales that used to keep little histories alive.

Now the place once so important in the affairs of Orange County is called the Seal Beach Naval Station. There is a plaque erected to keep alive dimming memories, but that's all.

An aging barber who knew Anaheim Landing when it was a place where people went to relax told me a little about it. It was largely a tent city in summer, although a few families built cabins. There, in the warm waters of a shallow bay, boys learned to swim.

My barber friend, Frank Dyer of Anaheim, remembered when he was a lad a ship had foundered in the bay. Boys of the era were most happy that the hulk never was refloated. Its dark interior was a playground and a dressing room for those planning to swim. It also provided a diving platform.

What ship was this that in death provided such boundless fun? I can find no record of the wreck. My barber friend is no longer here to tell me and I can find no other person who can recall the circumstances surrounding the tragedy.

Back in its early days Anaheim Landing was regarded as the future port for the area now composing Long Beach and southern Los Angeles. As a shipping point, it served a large area well. The German colonists who settled Anaheim hauled their wines to the Landing for shipment.

Lumber, hardware and farm implements were brought ashore there. Time and tides have changed all that.

Now the Navy has dredged a channel, probably over the place where the mystery ship broke apart in agony. The channel is neatly marked with stone levies.

All very efficient, which history is not. How much of this sort of history is lost forever we can never know. (May 5, 1964)

The Double Eagle

R ecently I fell to wondering:
Who in the nation today remembers the double eagle, that heavy cartwheel of gold whose possession once spelled a sense of well-being for the individual?

I know the answer, and it's a bit shocking. Let pass another decade or two and only a graying, wrinkled few will know what is meant by the name.

For those who never have held this monetary prize, let me explain that the double eagle was a $20 gold piece, almost an ounce of the precious stuff before revaluation was made mandatory under President Franklin Roosevelt's New Deal.

The $10 gold piece, called the eagle, carried the embossed image of a single proud eagle. Americans knew the $5 gold piece as a half eagle and the $2.50 coin as a quarter eagle. Some of these coins, legally squirreled away by coin collectors, are exhibited now on rare occasions.

When gold coins were removed from circulation I had a sense of personal loss that never has quite left me. I mourned a solid friend whose passing, I feared, signaled the end of an era.

Gold had been a heavy anchor against the winds and tides of inflation. At that time the argument was the anchor still would be there, and it would be more effective. Only those who knew and cherished the double eagle can judge that argument fully today.

The nation has managed without gold coins, of course, although there still are those who contend that progress would have been more solid and security more secure had gold been left in circulation.

The Double Eagle

As it is, comparatively little gold is being produced, especially in the United States. Only a few of the great mines are being worked. Official efforts discourage filing on mining claims, which is the prospector's legal way of protecting his discovery.

California, once a great gold-producing state, sees its mines idle because costs of production exceed the value of the product.

Gold, or the love of it, has been the cause of many of history's great and small tragedies. Whenever the glint of gold has appeared, even though it often has been only a miner's imagination, men have buckled on their pistols, some in greed, some for defense.

Jack Noble, one of the brothers who owned the Noble mines in San Diego County, spent his last years carrying a heavy revolver, and there are those who say he used it with lethal purpose against trespassers.

California's mountains and deserts hide the bones of many a prospector who lost his poke and his life to the god of greed.

I know all this, and still I would like to balance a double eagle on its milled edge, tap it gently with a lesser coin, and listen to its unforgettable resonance. (Feb. 26, 1963)

Scriptures Well Rooted

The United States Supreme Court has virtually ruled the Scriptures out of the nation's public schools, and pressure has been exerted to take from our coins a brief mention of the Deity.

But nothing the judges or the lawmakers can do ever will remove the Scriptures from our vocabulary. Each of us, almost daily, quotes the Bible, usually unconsciously.

Who has not asked, or thought, "Am I my brother's keeper?"

Who has not referred to a prosperous country as a "land flowing with milk and honey?"

The wisdom and the rhythm of the Old Testament authors merge easily into our daily conversations, bolstering our reasoning and giving force to our thoughts. We say sagely "man does not live by bread alone," but we seldom credit Mosaic Law with the quotation.

Few there are who have not repeated "the apple of his eye," another Mosaic bon mot.

"...quit yourselves like men," counseled Samuel, and a little later he said the Lord "sought men after His own heart." Who has not thought or spoken in these terms?

Remember "the still small voice?" Often we see the phrase in literature, but we seldom remember that it was the voice of the Lord after the earthquake and the fire recorded in I Kings.

Job spoke of the "king of terrors," and commented that "I am escaped with the skin of my teeth," phrases we use often because we know none more apt.

Scriptures Well Rooted

Dickens wrote "Twice Told Tales," paraphrasing the Psalmist who noted that: "we spend our lives as a tale that is told."

People often say they are "at their wit's end," seldom noting that they are quoting from a Psalm. Those who "go down to the sea in ships" are not New Englanders with sails unfurled; they were Mediterranean merchant men in King David's time.

"There is no new thing under the sun," observed Ecclesiastes, the Teacher. The same author commended men to "eat, drink and be merry." Sound familiar?

The idea that "the love of money is the root of all evil" comes from I Timothy.

Sometimes we attempt to improve on Scriptural phrasing. Job said, "How forceful are right words!" Mark Twain, polishing the same thought, said "The difference between the right word and the almost right word is the difference between lightning and a lightning bug."

Lesson in Ecology

My personal lesson in ecology has lasted the better part of a long lifetime. It began in 1901 when my father moved his family to Idaho's Nez Perce prairie.

He didn't go there for the attractions of a city, and there were few to be offered by the little trading center. He moved to Nez Perce because there was work to be had there — good paying work. It was harvest toil that paid my father five dollars a day. He received top pay because he could operate the engine in a threshing outfit, a type of work few men then were qualified to do.

The Nez Perce area hadn't been opened to settlers long. Indeed, there still were acres of lush bunch grass that hadn't been introduced to the plow. Land that had been tamed three or four years produced huge crops of wheat, oats and barley.

It was not uncommon for bluestem wheat to yield 50 bushels to the acre, and club wheat, a soft grain that could be planted in the spring, was good for 60 bushels. Oats and barley produced 80 and more bushels to the acre.

Farmers planted the same field year after year, giving the soil no rest. A few of the older farmers questioned the practice, but they did nothing about it. Most were certain that their good earth, a volcanic ash soil, had a strength that was inexhaustible.

They had a practice of burning the straw where it stood after the heads had been clipped. They did that to be rid of a nuisance at plowing time when straw left in the field would collect under the plow beam. When that happened the plowman had to stop and

get the accumulation out by hand.

Few ever thought of the straw as a priceless substance that the soil was begging to be returned to it. Burn it. Get it out of the way quickly.

Before many years there was an uneasiness among the more thoughtful farmers. Wheat production fell to 40 bushels to the acre, then to 30. They switched to less demanding types of wheat that produced well on shorter stalks.

But before I left the prairie 18 years later, hilltops had ceased to produce grain. Where I once had

plowed rich black soil there was grayish yellow clay. Russian and bull thistles had invaded the region and there was no stopping them.

When I last drove through the Nez Perce region, nearly 20 years ago, there no longer were houses and barns on each quarter section. The land for the most part was being operated by large corporations whose employees respected the land and who knew how to nurse it back into production. To me it was a sad sight, but it was good to learn that there were men who had gone to rescue the land. (Oct. 16, 1970)

Cost of Pollution

*T*here may be worse polluted streams than the south fork of Northern Idaho's Coeur d'Alene River, and there may be areas more devastated by industry than the once-beautiful canyon down which that river flows. I doubt it.

Time was when the Coeur d'Alene was one of the most beautiful rivers on earth. Clean and cold, it flowed through a wild region seen by few humans.

Then came the great silver-lead-zinc mines. Communities like Mullan, Wallace, Burke and Kellogg sprang up to provide services for the miners. They dumped raw sewage into the Couer d'Alene. Still worse, they dumped water from the ore mills into it — water that contained deadly potions of minerals.

Tailings, crushed rock from the mines, which had given up their riches, were poured onto the valley floor. Fish were killed. No animal could drink the water and live. Plant life watered by the river died.

There still was an abundance of lofty pines and firs on the canyon slopes.

Then I arrived. Not alone, but with several hundred other men, among them an engineer named W.K. Malette. He was there to build a smelter. My brother and I found work cutting a stand of young firs and brush from the smelter site.

Two years earlier we had worked at a mining and smelter operation in Washington state and had seen the sad results of toxic deposits on the surrounding area.

I had an opportunity to ask Malette if the smelter would destroy plant life in the canyon. Not at all, he assured me. Science had found a way to keep the sulfuric acid and other chemicals produced by smelters from escaping.

He said his engineers would do it with what was called the bag house, a tight building in which long bags made of wool were hung inverted from the ceiling. Furnace smoke entered the bottoms of the bags and filtered upward 30 feet before escaping up a tall chimney.

It didn't work. The bags captured some of the deadly material that otherwise would have been lost, but they did not entirely curb pollution.

I have been back to Kellogg several times since the smelter was "blown in" in 1918. The plant has grown and so has its shadow of death upon the environment. The canyon floor is many feet thick with black slag, the residue from the furnaces.

Prevailing winds have carried the fumes eastward up the canyon, killing virtually every tree and shrub for five miles or more. Few birds can be seen in the stricken area.

Farmers were the among the first to complain about the smelter's effect on valley crops in the early 1920's. Their pleas for relief went unanswered as mining interests argued their industry made a significant contribution to the state's and the nation's economy.

Some say the smelter is the life of the community. Others say the smelter is, or will be, the death of the community.

That's the way it is in Kellogg. (Feb. 23, 1970)

(Editor's Note: Federal and state agencies have begun the long and costly process of cleaning up the devastation wrought by 100 years of mining and smelter activity.

A large portion of the area around Kellogg has

been designated as the Bunker Hill Superfund Site, qualifying it for federal cleanup funds. Some restoration has taken place and more is planned.

About 2 million trees were planted by local football teams between 1980 and 1982. Tons of contaminated soils are being removed from properties in Kellogg and replaced with good earth.

Some environmental experts say it will take at least 50 years for the mountains and streams to recover.

Thousands of skiers now pass through Kellogg on their way to the highly acclaimed Silver Mountain ski area and the city is gradually turning to tourism as an alternate source of income.)

A Little Strawbuck

When I met Andy Riggins I was 10 years old. He was perhaps 50, although he may have been younger. In those days a man often seemed older than his years.

Andy was strawbuck on a threshing outfit on Idaho's Nez Perce prairie. His lowly task kept him in the chaff and straw much of the time. He was responsible for transporting waste from the separator to the engine, which consumed tons of the stuff in the making of steam.

I think Andy was paid $1.50 a day for his work, and it was a long day. For the services of his light team he probably got another 50 cents.

Andy Riggins was a little man, as harvest hands went. Lithe and wiry, he made up in wit and knowledge for what he lacked in weight. I often think he may have been a college man. Maybe not a graduate, but he had the bearing of a man of books, which rated him above his fellows in learning.

I don't recall that he ever used the vernacular of the men around him. He avoided the clipped "ain't," "hain't," and "youse" of his fellows without being accused of being stuck up.

He was the first person I ever heard use the phrase "circulating medium" when referring to money. I do not recall that he ever raised his voice among the crew where the loud voice was considered a mark of the leader.

He spoke of his "home" with something akin to pride. It was, he emphasized, a little difficult to reach, but well worth the effort. Home for Andy was on northern Idaho's defiant Salmon River. Nearby much big game was to be had and the streams abounded in trout, salmon and grayling.

From the stream beds it was possible to pan as much as $2.50 a day in gold dust, for his was gold country.

I think Andy probably made as much as $100 during the harvest season, which in those days lasted around 50 days. With that he bought his winter's groceries, heavy boots and clothing.

He emerged once a year from his mountain seclusion to be with people and get his winter stake.

Later Andy Riggins' name was fixed to a "town" which consists of a store, service station, motel, garage and a few residences. Through that town civilization has pushed Highway 95, stretching through Riggins, 125 miles north of Boise, and on to Canada. Riggins gets into the news when hunters get lost, hurt or worse.

It is, most of the time, a quiet monument to the little strawbuck from whom I learned the enchantment of words and ideas.

A Penny Saved

P eople do the darnedest things for money. Take me, for instance.

Many years ago I had completed work in the Northern Idaho harvest and wanted to return to my home in Clarkston, Wash., about 50 miles away. School wouldn't start for a week, but there was no more work for me in the fields. Thus time wasn't an element in my planning.

I did have a problem. I had taken my bicycle to the farming country. It was handy when I was looking for work and at the rare times when I needed to go to town. Now I had to get the bike back to my home.

The little railroad I planned to use for my journey wanted 50 cents for transporting the bicycle. In addition it wanted $3 for my ticket. That totaled as much as I had made for a whole day's work firing a traction engine.

So I decided to provide my own transportation. I would ride my bike home, even though the dirt roads were deep in autumn's dust. This was long before the light weight 10-speed wonders of today. I had one speed — slow.

Starting soon after noon, I pedaled to a little community called Winchester, arriving there about dark. I was tired and hungry. The town was ablaze with banners announcing a show to be given that night by a company of traveling actors.

I found the usual hotel accommodations were taken, but someone directed me to the home of a widow who, I was told, sometimes rented a room to travelers. Also she provided supper for those wanting it. For 50 cents she gave me a bounteous meal, which was served by her young daughters, giggling girls about 14 and 16 years old. The room also was 50 cents.

Declining an invitation to go to the show, I was directed to my room at the top of a narrow stairs. There was no door where a door should have been. Instead a blanket hung over the opening.

The room had unmistakable signs of femininity. The rough dressing table was covered with such things as a comb, a hand mirror, powder puff and hairpins. There was a fragrance that told me the girls had surrendered their room for my use.

I had a featherbed that night, the last one I ever slept upon. The widow and the girls went to the show and I dimly remember that I heard them return home around 11 o'clock. I don't know where they slept.

Next morning they served me a breakfast of ham, eggs, coffee and browned potatoes for which they charged 35 cents.

I still had 30 miles to ride my bike to reach home, but I had the satisfaction of having saved more than $2 that went to support me in school that winter.

Crop of Idioms

*I*n addition to the food and fiber supplied by farms, agriculture and allied pursuits have contributed rich additions to our language. They have given us a great variety of picturesque idioms and figures of speech that creep into every-day conversations.

Much of this legacy has come to us from the Bible, the first record we have of the tiller of the soil.

Who has not compared some individual with the "lost sheep" of the Scriptures? Who has not described the actions of some acquaintance as "sowing seeds among thorns?"

And there is the oft-repeated admonition that a man having "put his hand to the plow should not look back."

Youth today often is advised that his harvest will depend upon the seed he sows. Teachers constantly seek to "plant ideas," a phrase that comes straight from the soil.

Speaking of the soil, how often do we say that our clothes or hands are "soiled"?

From the farm comes the idiomatic admonition to "bridle our passions."

The farm also provided the unwholesome excuse that "youth must sow its wild oats".

Society is liberally endowed with people said to be "stubborn as a mule," or "dumb as an ox."

From the barnyard comes the advice not to be a "pig" and the simile "eats like a hog."

Chances are that our language never will divorce itself from "bringing home the bacon," an apt term that describes accomplishment.

"Small potatoes" accurately describes some

persons as well as their objectives and attainments. Closely allied with that phrase is the description of the man who produces a small "crop of ideas." And how about: "He's growing like a weed"? People who never have been nearer to horses than a race track will advise others to "plow deep" for new ideas.

I like one figure of speech that seldom is heard today. My father used to approach a difficult task with the declaration that he would "bust a hamestring" trying to achieve results. Perhaps this phrase failed to endure because few people know what a hamestring is.

Hames are the essential parts of a harness for a horse. They fit around the collar which enables the horse to "put his shoulder to the wheel" or to the plow.

There are two hames to each harness. Made of strong oak reinforced with steel, they are held in place by tough, adjustable leather straps called traces or "hamestrings." The "busting" of a hamestring signified supreme effort.

We could continue our "harvest" of idioms, but as they say down on the farm: enough is enough.

Tastes of Youth

My father thought in 1893 that he was leaving Indiana, but he misjudged the strength of the state of his birth. He never got Indiana out of himself.

Once in the West (near Salem, Oregon), he longed for some of the things he remembered fondly about Indiana. Things like maple syrup and sorghum molasses.

He also revered the memory of the Kentucky squirrel rifle my grandfather had bought to protect his farm against the imagined threat of invaders. But I think the taste of maple syrup and sorghum clung most tenaciously.

The region of his new home had an abundance of maple trees, so he decided to show the old timers a thing or two. They said Oregon maple would not produce sap that would boil down into syrup.

We had a large cast iron kettle. I remember it as 40-gallon capacity.

In February and March the sap was running strong. Father put out his buckets and had no difficulty collecting enough sap for a trial run.

For the better part of a week we kept a fire going under the kettle, daily adding buckets of sap.

As time passed, gloom settled over the experiment. The sap boiled down, but what remained in the kettle was not syrup. There simply was no sugar in it.

Oh, it was slightly sweet, but there was more bitterness than sweetness to the taste.

Father finally dipped out about a quart — a stingy reward for his labor.

He conceded to the Oregon old-timers.

It took much longer to get the longing for

sorghum out of his mind.

He tried the product obtainable from the grocer's shelves, but it never tasted quite right.

Eventually he came to make his home with my family in Orange County. We learned of a man — Sorghum Sprout, he was called — living nearby who had a cane field and made sorghum. We bought a couple of quarts from him.

I believe it was one of father's greatest disappointments. What he missed was not Indiana sorghum; what was lacking were the taste buds of his youth.

Friend Sorely Missed

*A*fter 28 years of constant companionship, I have lost a friend to whom (or to which) I want to pay tribute. This friend didn't die, or pass away. "Lost" is the correct word for what happened, although that doesn't do the story justice.

This friend has seen me through many trials and tribulations never complaining of slight, always helping me when possible, a comfort and a strong reed to lean upon.

For instance, my friend has stood by me through many minor bits of surgery. When I have had briers to remove from fingers, or a splinter to lift out, I did not have to do the task alone. My friend was there, ready, willing and able.

On occasion my friend has joined me in such boyish delights as making whistles from green willows.

At times I have needed skilled help while repairing my car. Without the aid of this friend I would have been sorely tried when stripping the insulation from ignition wires. At other times I could not have cut a leader for fishing tackle without my friend's help.

When engaged in crude mending that I set myself to do, my friend has helped me get thread and needle into a proper relationship.

While it never was necessary for me to call upon my friend for any acts of self defense, I have been strengthened in my resolves just to know I was not alone in difficult situations.

It seems strange, too, that my friend helped me keep good discipline over my own inclinations. For

101

instance, I seldom permitted my trouser pockets to develop holes. The instant I noted signs of weakened fabric, I got busy with my mending chores.

He was sharp and came quickly to the point. He looked after my pencils to be sure they were properly sharpened. That was a chore I appreciated because I abhor those pencil sharpeners that have invaded offices under the guise of progress.

My friend's family name was Case, a family long engaged in the manufacture of fine cutlery, but I called him Jack K.

Withal, my friend was a companion I could depend upon, always ready, never in the way. Our friendship was honed by 28 years of togetherness.

I know I shall miss him greatly, and it grieves me deeply to know I shall have to dig deep into my wallet to acquire another friend to serve me as well.

The lost friend cost me $4. Yesterday I found one exactly like him in a hardware store. The merchant's price was $7.65.

"Good jackknives are expensive," he said, unabashed. "And the one you hold is very good." (May 13, 1970)

Calabasas

The first time I saw Calabasas, on the eastern side of the Santa Monica Mountains, I was in search of a story.

It was renowned as the hiding place of desperadoes. Horse thieves, cattle rustlers, robbers — yes, and murderers — went into hiding there in the brush-covered mountains. It was safe for them because only one road entered from the east and one from the west.

I went in from the west, starting where the mountains dip their toes into the cooling Pacific Ocean, and climbed almost to the pinnacle, nearly 3,000 feet.

I didn't get my story, but I did get something sweet.

I got honey. That honey was almost as clear as mountain spring water. It was made from the nectar of nothing but mountain sage, the growth that recently fed raging fires.

The region produced that honey because it is swept almost nightly by cooling breezes that bring dense fog off the ocean. Almost as wet as rain, the fog kept the sage in bloom for months after other mountain areas became summer deserts.

Apiarists had discovered their bees could work for long periods without having to move their hives to new blossom areas.

I bought some of that honey. It cost $1.25 a gallon then.

I wonder now if the honey dealer's stand still is there beside the narrow road. I wonder if the scout bees sent out from each hive still find ample sage blossoms for their product.

Calabasas

Life for a bee must be rather dreary if it finds nothing but ashes where there had been flowers. Reporters covering the recent fires did not mention the fate of the bees.

Perhaps only sweet memory will rise from the ashes. (Nov. 12, 1973)

The Ridge Route

*H*istory, like the passing of the old Ridge Route over the Tehachapi Mountains and the development of a new one, has a way of catching up with a man.

I knew the old Ridge Route when it was young.

As a paved highway it was only four years old when we became acquainted, and the introduction was a lesson in how to drive over one of the most winding, most tortuous grades then in existence.

It was early November, 1923, when with my bride I came to California. We had come from Washington where we thought our mountains were the highest (they weren't), the roughest, and the most beautiful. We thought real mountains had to be tree covered. (They don't).

In Tacoma we had heard of the Ridge Route, 43.2 miles of dizzy mountain trail. Drivers returning from California praised the route, even as they remembered the grades, the curves and the switchbacks that made it, at one and the same time, an engineering marvel and a highway to be avoided by the timid.

Not many trucks then used the highway. A number of vehicles failed to make the curves and rolled to the bottom of steep canyons to become statistics.

The highway, then, as now, climbed to 4,245 feet to creep through Tejon Pass, once the route for the camel trains used to supply troops at Ft. Tejon.

From the pass it writhed eastward a mile or so, then took off down a barren shale ridge with twists and turns that frightened some and challenged all Los

Angeles-bound drivers. It has been recorded that there were 100 complete circles in the 43 miles of roadway.

The route mainly followed those wind-swept ridges, dodging from one ridge across canyons to another. I do not recall there was a single service station from the high point on the route to the bottom of the grade. Drivers needed plenty of gas and a full load of luck when they undertook the trip.

Later, service stations were built, along with motels, although they weren't called that then. It was at one of those tourist accommodations that U.S. Grant Jr., builder of San Diego's U.S. Grant Hotel, died in his sleep the night of Sept. 29, 1929.

The Ridge Route soon was unable to handle the traffic that had developed between Los Angeles and the San Joaquin Valley. In 1935, if memory serves me right, I was invited to a ribbon-cutting that opened the second Ridge Route. It was such an improvement that no one thought it eventually would have to be replaced, but it has.

And what is more, engineers already are beginning to wonder how long the new highway's eight lanes will carry all the cars and trucks that will demand space on them. (Nov. 30, 1970)

Frontier Justice

A few of California's once-bustling frontier towns cling stubbornly, and perhaps pridefully, to an institution once renowned for its effectiveness as an instrument of justice.

That is the hangman's tree, sometimes referred to as the court of last resort or the Old West's version of a suspended sentence.

Recently one of these ancient reminders, the Hangman's Tree of Calabasas, itself suffered the extreme indignity of execution. It was condemned by progress. The tree stood beside a highway, constricting the road so that a Saturn II missile could not be trucked away from its birthplace in the Santa Susana Mountains, north of Los Angeles.

But there are communities where the hangman's tree is an attraction preserved to provide a shudder for the passing tourist.

San Diego may have had one or more such trees, although it seems probable that the pioneer populace of this city was not partial. Any old handy tree seems to have been acceptable, and there were occasions when a strong limb and a lariat served what loosely was called society in the early days.

Twice in Richard Pourade's volume "The Glory Years," the demise of an evildoer in this grim court is recorded. Perhaps the trees long ago fell victims to the woodcutter's ax.

One of the finest specimens of such trees is a

huge juniper in Holcomb Valley, about five miles north of Big Bear Lake.

This tree, probably 75 feet tall and four feet through at the base, extends a stout limb parallel to the earth and perhaps 25 feet above the ground. Here, William Carley, an early observer of the Holcomb Valley mining camp, noted that of "50 to 60 men who were killed (by hanging on the tree), not more than five or six were innocent".

Orange County has its hangman's tree, a spreading sycamore in Santiago Canyon. Two members of the murderous Juan Flores gang came to a hasty end there nearly a century ago. The tree is carefully preserved.

The real kingdom of the hangman's tree was the gold mining region of Northern California, where gnarled old oaks still stand in mute testimony that bad men once met their reward there. Placerville once had one of these trees, but as the city grew the site was needed for a street.

Chinese Camp's hanging tree stood on ground so laden with gold that the tree became an obstacle to the acquisition of wealth. It was dug out long ago.

Sutter Creek and Sonora each had what are described as "active trees." Big Oak Flats had an oak that was too high for the rope tosser who had to cast the noose over a limb. It was abandoned for a smaller tree.

Indeed, hardly a frontier community of the West passed through its infant stage without a hanging tree, an institution now regarded by some with a sense of pride. (Oct. 5, 1965)

Rules of Decorum

During my lifetime in newspaper offices our language has undergone some startling changes, maybe for the better; I don't know.

When I began my first job as a reporter in 1918 I often was troubled by problems of expression because of rules we worked under. There were words we simply did not write into our news reports.

An angry man might say, "I want you to quote me exactly as I say it. I don't give a .... what the district attorney says." That's the way we had to write it, and I assume no reader missed the intent or the meaning.

The district attorney (we called him the prosecuting attorney in our state) might respond, "You tell our friend to go to ....", a rejoinder that had all the force of a busted balloon. Sometimes we varied our reporting by using innocuous dashes instead of periods to get the ideas across.

Our editors in those days were prone to the birds-and-bees expressions. There was a general recognition that sex does exist, but we did not mention the fact in our reports. A woman might be referred to as "in a delicate condition," but never in the exact terms found in news reports today.

While our editors recognized the evils, legal and moral, that beset our community, we avoided use of words that are common to news stories now.

It was correct for us to refer to cows, feminine gender, but we tried to avoid calling attention to their bellowing husbands, though this was not an absolute verboten. It just wasn't nice to drag bulls into a news story if it could be avoided.

Rules of Decorum

Such subjects as illegitimacy, abortion and family planning, common in today's newspapers and magazines, were discussed only behind closed doors, and they were not reported in the press.

Today it seems that the dictionary is the limit — and what a limit! The modern editions contain most of the words we were told to shun. Perhaps this is on the assumption that everyone knows the words anyway. Whether these words creep into conversations is up to the users of the dictionary.

I assume all this change in usage can be blamed on the wars we have had during my lifetime. Young men who were reared in sheltered homes shared experiences easiest described in strong words. Often they had neither time nor inclination to choose the niceties of expression.

Motion pictures and the bang-bang novelists reporting on wars were more realistic than were my early editors.

And thus we have reversed direction in our vocabulary, and are back about where Shakespeare was, or maybe a bit farther back. (Oct. 1, 1963)

Bolt From Blue

Nature's efforts to keep humanity on the defense often are frightening, but never more so than when the attack takes the form of fire. I say this after experiences with flood, quake and flames.

People usually can swim or perhaps get a boat in time of flood. Often there is time to prepare, though not always. Earthquakes strike without warning, but, unless the victims are caught by the first terrifying temblor, survival for most is a reasonable certainty.

But fire, now. It can come with a bolt of lightning. Summer clouds often are the terrible couriers for an attack, like the time in 1925 when a dagger of light struck an oil tank at what was known as the Brea tank farm in Orange County.

From a distance of 6 miles I had watched clouds gathering over the hills back of Brea, vaguely suspecting they carried the potential for trouble. I had a reporter in Brea who would call me if anything unusual happened, I thought.

There were sharp clashes of thunder and brilliant displays of lightning that zig-zagged across the sky. It seemed unlikely any of those shafts of crackling power could become newsworthy, but one did.

This particular bolt broke from an ominous cloud and struck one of the oil-filled tanks in the 40-acre tank farm. There were perhaps a dozen tanks, each designed to hold 25,000 barrels of crude oil.

The lightning struck a tank at the upper edge of the hillside cluster. There was an instant flash as the electric charge touched the blanket of gas resting over the oil and started a fire that lasted more than a week.

At first only one tank was affected. As the oil burned on the surface it heated the tank into a boiling cauldron. At times the flames died down as if resting, then burst forth with greater fury.

The oil overflowed the steel tank and spilled down the hillside, a river of fire that ignited other tanks.

There was no way to fight the flames, except to starve them.

The farm was connected by an 8-inch pipe to another cluster of tanks in San Pedro, about 30 miles away. Oil was drained as rapidly as possible from the bottoms of the burning tanks and pumped to San Pedro. The liquid became so hot there were fears it would ignite in the pipe, perhaps shooting flames all the way to the coast.

It was terrifying. It was destructive. Eventually the flames became weary and died.

And my reporter? She had missed the story of the year in Brea because, she explained, she was afraid to use the telephone during the electrical storm.

Gratitude Endures

Recently Roy Hofheinz, a Texas millionaire, bought the Ringling Bros. Circus, paying $10 million for the outfit.

Deals of that magnitude are not unusual in this age of high finance. But this one was out of the ordinary because it involved enduring sentimental values.

Hofheinz once was a newspaper boy who had to make his earnings count. When possible, he saved a few dimes and when he had enough, he held them until a circus came to his city, then he would take his mother.

It was the most impressive thing he could do to reward her for the home she strove to provide for him.

But the rest of the time he saw the circuses only from the outside. Hanging around the big tents, he sometimes got glimpses of the animals and the circus people he admired.

As time passed, he gained in years, in respect among his fellows and in wealth. He served as a judge, as a legislator, as a mayor. His money came from oil investments, television and radio.

There this sentimental story might end, except for the late Sam Kramer of Placentia, whom I met many years ago.

Sam was around 80 years old at the time of our meeting. He had just completed construction of a handsome six-story bank and office building, the tallest in old Anaheim. I wanted to know why he had chosen to build such a structure in the depths of the Depression.

As with Mr. Hofheinz, the story went back to his youth when his father was a sheepman in what became the Placentia area. Sam's job was to herd the flocks on the dry hills his father owned. There was little opportunity to get an education, and Sam got almost none.

Nor was there much chance to enjoy sports and adventure as other boys did.

But there was one thing in all the years that made his life worthwhile.

On Fourth of July holidays he had the day off. Then he would don clean overalls and walk barefoot to Anaheim for the celebration.

The oratory, the parade, the athletic events thrilled him. They gave him a feeling there was something in life beyond the shepherd's lot.

As the years passed drillers discovered a vast deposit of oil under the barren hills he inherited. Orange growing on his land became profitable.

Sam kept busy developing the property his father had left to him, and in rearing a family of which he was proud.

But he never forgot the pleasures Anaheim had given him at a time of life when prospects for improvement were dim.

Indeed, it is good to know that some men do not forget. (Jan. 2, 1968)

Sheep Deserve Better

I never could comprehend the low regard some folks hold for the sheep industry. Such people refer to the sheep herder in terms that often are less then complimentary, a habit that displays ignorance, I believe.

Sheep and shepherds deserve better.

Sheep had a sizable role in settling the West. They provided a nucleus of the funds that were spent by the Bixby family in founding Long Beach.

The name Bixby is honored throughout California, and yet I knew one member of the family who spent lavishly of her funds to direct public attention away from the sheep that did so much for her forebears.

The name Bastanchury means something special in Orange County where Basque sheepmen a century ago purchased a large acreage for pasturing their flocks. Discovery of oil on the property did much to wipe out the lowly record of the sheep business, and today it seldom is mentioned.

In the columns of The San Diego Union, dated 1870, there is an item about the arrival of a flock of sheep that had been driven from the Midwest to provide food for the community. San Diegans were happy to get that mutton.

Sheep raising once was of considerable importance in San Diego County. Indeed, as late as 1968, the county produced 45,000 pounds of wool. However, by 1969, wool production had declined to a meager three tons.

There is something that cannot be overlooked in assessing the decline of sheep culture in the Southland. Sheep are not highly regarded by cattlemen. They look upon them as an abomination, and there is some reason for that attitude.

Sheep have small feet — small compared to the weight of the animal. Those small hooves cut into and pack the turf so that grass roots do not thrive.

Moreover, sheep graze closer to the soil than do cattle, thus destroying the plants. It has been alleged this feeding habit contributes to erosion.

That much can be said against sheep, and yet there are areas of the West where sheep and sheepmen are highly regarded.

Nevada, I have discovered, honors its Basques, a people who came from the Pyrenees region of Spain to tend sheep on the state's plains. Each year Nevadans gather, dressed in the colorful costumes of the Pyrenees, to sing and dance to honor the Basques.

It is a small tribute to pay those who endure the loneliness of life with their faithful dogs and their flocks.

Gasoline Shortage

G asoline famine is nothing new to the American motorist.

In 1920 there were virtually no gas stations and those we had were often closed. Of course, there were not many cars, either.

Many a farmer still relied on what he called his "hay burner." But those who had cars were sorely tried when the fuel tank ran dry.

There was one way to keep a car going, which I looked on with some doubt and trepidation. When there was no gas to be had, we would pour in five gallons of kerosene and add a quart of what I remembered as carbon tetrachloride, which we could get from a drug store.

Usually, the method worked, but there was no assurance that it would. Sometimes it blew the engine head off. Sometimes the engine simply wouldn't start on the mixture.

If the engine did start, there was no assurance it wouldn't stop unexpectedly. And there was almost a certainty the power would be jumpy and uneven.

That was in the period when Signal Hill and Huntington Beach were being discovered. At the time, there was an abundance of oil, but the refining and distributing facilities had not been developed. A little later Santa Fe Springs came to our rescue.

At the time of the shortage, the main highway between Tacoma and Seattle was a two-lane brick-surfaced design, called the "Valley Line." I used to entertain myself by counting the cars I would meet driving between the two cities.

That road has been all but abandoned, and two

new highways have replaced it. Only a computer could count the traffic on those thoroughfares now.

Fifty years ago, the man who had a car was the exception. Today, the man who has no car is the exception, and indeed the man who has only one car is the real exception. We travel more. We waste more miles. And use more gasoline. (Sept. 15, 1973)

Bill Noonan, Genius

My list of meanings contains two definitions for the word "genius."

First, there is the common meaning that includes the man who can do something extraordinary, perhaps something no other person has done, and specially something beneficial to mankind.

Thus Samuel Morse, inventor of the telegraph, was a genius, but John Dillinger, super bandit, was not.

Then there is the other meaning, which I like better. It applies to the person who does his or her job better than anyone else. Such a person was Bill Noonan, a telegraph operator I knew in the early 1920's.

Noonan was one of two operators who, wearing headsets, "took" coded news off the wires for sister newspapers in Tacoma. Bill was on duty six and sometimes seven days a week for the morning newspaper while Vic Miller took the report for the afternoon paper.

Both of these men were excellent operators. They had to be if they were to interpret the dots and dashes at the speed the signals were sent. Bill was especially skilled.

Vic was an older man who had learned to receive the report on a Remington typewriter. It was a machine that did not permit the operator to see what he had typed, unless he paused and lifted the platen. Of simple design, Vic's typewriter was less likely to get out of order than were the modern machines of the day.

Bill typed steadily eight hours a day, rarely

making an error. The news came in at the rate of 35 to
37 words a minute, using the Associated Press code, a
system that required the operator to fill in missing
words. The abbreviations were expanded into complete sentences.

When Vic was typing he absolutely refused to
permit anyone to speak to him.

Bill did not mind being spoken to when receiving. He could carry on a conversation while recording
the news.

That was remarkable, but he had another
achievement that marked him for a place in my memory. While he was typing the news, he would read the
Saturday Evening Post.

He was a man of infinite energy. Usually he
came to work at 1 p.m., but he already had done a half
day's work transcribing a court reporter's notes.
Usually the reporter dictated his notes onto a
Dictaphone record, but sometimes Bill was unable to
understand the dictation. In order to overcome that
problem he learned to read the reporter's shorthand.

Bill's favorite recreation was on the golf course
where he probably could have made his mark as a
professional if he had wanted to.

I don't know what happened to Bill when the
high-speed Teletype printers displaced him, but I feel
certain he never lacked for a job.

Privilege or Rights?

Viewing society as it is today, I wonder whether we have been wise in adopting so many new devices, such as Social Security, welfare and the unbalanced budget.

My position on this is not entirely stand-offish. I like that monthly check and other benefits. However, it is a stance taken with some thought to the future.

I have noticed in my own case that once I have expanded my standards of living I have great difficulty in returning to old standards, if it appears to be necessary.

Take the matter of transportation. I got along quite well for a number of years without a bicycle, although I wanted one very much. After I had become accustomed to one, I looked upon it as evidence of a right.

The same situation prevailed when I acquired a car. Sure, I wanted one several years before I succumbed, but once I had a steering wheel in my hand — and a loan to pay off — I defended my privilege as a right.

Some years later I had to sell my car at a time when a replacement was impossible. During a long summer I walked or rode the buses. It was galling, but not unbearable.

The same situation prevailed at my table. Before the days of the Depression I bought food for my home without thinking much about the cost. I came to regard the best as none too good for my family.

Thus it was difficult to adjust downward to a Depression diet that sometimes consisted of large bowls of potato soup. But I did adjust.

Now I join, mentally at least, with those who demand more Social Security and we get it. I demand more Medicare, and if I don't get it, I am rebellious.

My car may spew the makings of smog, but I resent the suggestion that I should get rid of it. My rights are at issue.

My attitude, and that of my neighbors, springs from the ease with which we tap the nation's treasury. It doesn't matter that the treasury is empty, or worse, we tap it anyway.

What's the difference? I am not going to have to repay the bill, I tell myself deceitfully.

Actually, though, we already are being penalized for that policy. We pay higher prices for the food we eat and the clothes we wear. It costs more to operate our cars. When the pressure on our purses becomes too great, we tap the U.S. Treasury again.

That explains my apprehension about venturing into costly new social experiments. (July 16, 1971)

Pun Can Be Fun

Writing jokes for a living can be a serious matter, if not an exercise in futility.

Take my recent attempt to use a catchy little tag line I had dreamed up. It was obvious that it required a little knowledge of history, of geography and of the animal life of the region I selected.

Those three fields of knowledge placed the locale for my joke in one specific place — Egypt. It wouldn't be fun in any other locale, and even then it was no knee slapper.

Having decided that much, I wrote: "What would an Egyptian boy say if he fell into the Nile amid a 'flock' of crocodiles?"

I knew that was wrong; any joke book editor would read no further.

Would it be better to say a "herd" of crocodiles, or perhaps a "gang"?

That led me to some research where I found there is a special vocabulary for congregations of animals.

Turtles, which like crocodiles, are reptiles, are called "bales" when they get together. Thus a convention of turtles would be called a "bale."

Geese gather in "gaggles," but only if they are in water; in flight a gaggle of geese becomes a "skein." Don't ask me why; I'm only telling what my research revealed.

I think rhinoceroses have the most appropriate name for their group, a "crash."

Whales and dolphins swim in a "pod." In New England a pod of whales is known as a "gam." Maybe I can make something of that sometime.

I haven't the foggiest notion why a group of wolves should be called a "rout," but it is. However, I can imagine why an aggregation of goldfinches should be called a "charm."

Having this information did me no good. There is nothing I could find to help me with crocodiles.

So I returned to my tag line. What DID the little boy say when he fell into the River Nile?

"I want my mummy."

Fire!

S uppose you awoke in the night and found flames destroying your house. There would not be much time to make a choice of what to save.

Children of course. No one would forget them. But after them, what?

Pets come high on the list. Mature people have lost their lives trying to save a cat or a bird.

After that, the choice would be wide. What an otherwise intelligent person will drag from the flames sometimes is ludicrous if not ridiculous.

I once knew a man who awoke to find a large lumber yard and mill burning within a block of his home. It seemed that nothing could save his property.

The next thing he remembered was standing beside a five-gallon crock of eggs that was "put down" in a preservative called water glass. He had carried the crock a half block. Fortunately, his house did not burn.

A woman I knew fled from her burning house, carrying an almost valueless heavily framed painting of her great grandfather. Everything else she owned was destroyed.

I believe a man is more likely to think of money than a woman. With that he can meet the immediate needs of his family if all else is lost.

However, one man I read about left his money to burn while he carried out his hunting rifle. Another man escaped from his smoke-filled home, then ran back for his guns and died when the house exploded.

The human mind may not function normally during such unexpected emergencies. An individual may not consider the value or the usefulness of what he saves, like the man who grabbed his huge stuffed sail fish off the wall and carried it triumphantly to safety.

Early in life, I learned that horses are even more confused than are their owners when fire rages around their stalls. Open the door and they will refuse to be led to a safe place.

If they are forced to leave the stable, they will race back to their stalls if chance offers.

We were taught how to meet such emergencies. Simply tie a coat, sweater or grain sack across the animal's eyes, grab the halter and lead it to safety.

As for myself, I doubtless would save some silly and useless trinket, but on second thought, maybe not. I believe I would grab a 40-pound box of snapshots and family pictures as I crawled through the bedroom window, although I don't know why. I almost never look at them.

Dog's View of Home

Some dogs, I believe, have an uncanny sense of home. Not just a place on a map where home is; it is more than that. Home to these animals means people. It means the love of children, and it means security.

It took two mongrel dogs from the same general area of the United States to give credence to this theory.

One was a pet called Salty. Her family, thinking to do her a kindness, gave her away. Her new home, it was hoped, would be in an area where she could run and bark without disturbing neighbors.

It was 300 miles away.

But Salty missed the people she had known. So she took off and last week — three months later — limped into the place in Detroit that had meant everything to her. Though foot sore and weary, her wagging tail told everyone she was happy. Never again would Salty be given away, her owners vowed.

Strange as that may sound, it falls short of the exploits of a dog I met in Anaheim 30 years ago. The dog's name was Duke. There was nothing about Duke to distinguish him from thousands of other dogs. He had a short nose, short course hair, and an abiding love for his family.

Duke's home had been in Wisconsin. When his master made plans to move the family west the dog presented a problem. In a car packed with luggage there would be no room for Duke. Finally he was given to a neighbor.

After a few weeks Duke disappeared from his new home. No one of record saw him until he stumbled, lame and nearly starved, to his family's new home in California. It had taken him five months to reach the people who meant so much to him. The distance was 2,000 miles.

The finding of his friends meant more to him than food. Not until he had greeted every member of the household was he ready for the meal set before him.

Duke never had been out of his home state before being given away. There was nothing in the knowledge of man that could have guided him. His food problem must have been difficult, but we could only guess. Someone must have fed him along the way, but no one ever offered him an acceptable substitute for what he was seeking — the love he associated with home.

When I met him he was relaxing on the front porch of his home, chin resting on his outstretched paws, eyes worshipfully watching the man who had treated him so shabbily in Wisconsin. No recriminations, no hard feelings. We could tell by the way he wagged his tail. (Jan. 21, 1971)

Bomb Shelters

*I*t has been several years since I have read about those bomb shelters that once were so popular in many cities. It seems only yesterday that San Diegans were digging holes in their back yards or turning basements into places to hide, if they had basements.

The idea was that if a warning siren sounded, shelter owners would rush to the holes they had dug, close a trap door and wait out an expected attack. They had bunks, a cupboard stocked with food and enough bottles of water to last those in the "party" for a week or 10 days.

If there were children in the family, games were provided. For older persons there were books. Many had generators for electric lighting and some even had air conditioning.

At one time there was a suggestion that a huge cavern be dug for the convenience of downtown workers. Civil defense planners proposed to hollow out the point of land on which El Cortez Hotel stands. (That was long before Interstate 5 cut through the area.)

As many as 35,000 people could have found shelter there in an emergency, the planners estimated.

A little time and arithmetic dashed that idea. It was assumed that no more than 20 minutes would be allowed for people to get from their offices into the shelter.

How would 35,000 individuals get down elevators and into the shelter within that time?

Then there was the problem of assembling and storing food and water. Who was going to pay for all that? Beds had to be provided, too.

Bomb Shelters

Thus the idea died aborning, but the digging of garden variety shelters lived on for some time.

In those days we lived in East San Diego where I had ample room for a cave, but digging was so difficult in the rock-filled adobe soil that I quickly decided not to dig a hole big enough for my wife and me. It would have had to be cement lined, made water proof and stocked with food.

And besides, if bombs were to fall I wanted to be out where I could see what was going on, and I suspect that other non-diggers had the same idea.

Often I wonder what happened to all those caves that were dug and stocked with supplies. Were they filled in and lawns planted over them? Are they still there, awaiting the day when shelter diggers may say: "I told you so"?

Fuel Crisis in '49

*I*n January of 1949 residents of our East San Diego neighborhood came within 20 minutes of being offered meals of beef stew, and it would have been their only hot meals for several days.

Here is how it came about:

A series of bitterly cold nights had caused house-holders to turn their heaters up full blast. At that time the San Diego Gas & Electric Co. had but one gas line to bring fuel to the city from the main Texas-to-California line. The SDG&E pipe connected with the main line near Hemet.

Officials of the company became alarmed when pressures went down. They used the newspapers and radio to inform consumers that if consumption was not reduced it would be necessary to deprive large sections of the city of gas. That meant valves would be turned off.

After that happened there would be no service until every appliance in the affected area had been visited twice by company workmen.

The first workman would turn off every appliance in every home in the area. Afterward another would return to "bleed" the air from the lines. The operation would have lasted several days.

Reduce your heat, the company pleaded, and fortunately San Diegans cooperated.

The late Lawrence Klauber, gas company president, said to me later:

"We were within 15 to 20 minutes of being forced to halt service. That would have been a genuine disaster. I never have carried such a burden, and I determined that, cost what it would, it never would happen again."

The company began at once to build another gas line from Hemet, and to install gas storage facilities. One such facility is on the mesa north of Mission Valley; another is in the Encanto area.

At the time the crisis appeared unavoidable, our home on 40th Street near El Cajon Boulevard had in the kitchen a 16-quart kettle. More important, we had a stove that burned wood.

We held a conference and came to a decision.

If the gas was shut off we would make a stew (in my Army days we called it slum or mulligan). People would be invited to come for a warm meal. We had all the ingredients for a lot of stew and probably could have fed more than a hundred.

Fortunately, gas users reduced the heat in their homes, and pressure began to build up in the system. The crisis was over.

Since that distant date, the city's gas supply has been increased and my wife and I have moved to another community where our home is heated by electricity. We have disposed of our big kettle and the little wood-burning stove.

I'm a little sorry we missed an opportunity to share a tasty stew with our neighbors. It would have been fun. (Jan. 24, 1971)

Humor Slightly Singed

*E*ven if Chief Joe Shermann were still alive (he passed to a fire-eater's reward several months ago) I doubt that I could learn whether he had a real sense of humor.

You'd have to know Joe to understand, and perhaps this little story from years past will illustrate.

Joe Shermann spent a long and useful life as head of the Orange County Fire Department, a job that required that he and his crew hurry, siren wailing, to the scene of any rural fire in the county.

As I remember, they had one piece of rolling equipment, a red fire wagon that was a combination pumper and chemical suppression unit. Their station was in the city of Orange.

One wintry evening I had settled down for a restful hour before turning in for the night. As I sat reading, I remembered something I wanted to discuss with my friend Lee Deming (he's gone, too) and I went to the phone, little suspecting the drama that awaited me.

Mrs. Deming answered:

"Oh, my house is on fire. Lee isn't here. What shall I do?"

I advised her to call Joe Shermann, who was some 10 miles distant. I promised to hurry to the Deming home, about four miles out among the orange groves west of Anaheim.

Mrs. Deming met me at the door and led me into a large newly painted room. There was smoke, all right. It was seeping from an electrical outlet box in the ceiling. There surely was fire behind the metal box cover.

I found the switch box and turned off the current. Now I was in darkness, but a flashlight helped. There was a three-gallon fire extinguisher handy, and I brought it into the room. With a screw driver I opened the electrical outlet box. Immediately there were flames. The box had been so tight that it had not permitted the smoldering rafters to flare up.

The fire extinguisher soon had the fire under control.

(I found later that a painter had just redone the room and had twisted the electric wires, causing a short.)

By this time I heard Joe's fire wagon clanging. I ran into the road and flagged down the rig.

"The fire's out," I announced proudly. "I got it with a fire extinguisher."

Just to be sure, Joe thought he would take a look.

Convinced his services were not needed, he said, not smiling at all:

"Shucks, what did you do that for? We would've been here before the house was half burned down."

See what I mean?

A Costly Habit

My drinking habits should bring joy to those Colombian mountain-valley people who produce the aromatic coffee berry. The Associated Press reported recently that I, being an average man, drink an average of 800 cups of the brew a year, and that should perk up the growers' welfare quite a bit.

Actually it may not help much after all. I suspect the money I contribute toward their income gets spread around a lot before it reaches the grower.

I was startled this week to discover that I pay at the rate of $1,820 a ton for the coffee I buy. Of course I don't buy a ton at a time, and if I did the price might be slightly lower.

My habit is to buy a one-pound can, hermetically sealed, for which I pay 91 cents. That amount insures me of at least 45 cups of good brew that costs me about 2 cents a cup.

If I order a cup of coffee in a restaurant, and nothing more, it's certain to cost a dime, and possibly twice that. Even at 10 cents a cup, it would cost $4.55 to buy a pound of coffee converted into steaming beverage.

As a confirmed coffee drinker I acknowledge a debt to some Arabian goats for discovering the berry. It happened 1,120 years ago. A goat-herder named Kaldi noticed his herd seemed especially exhilarated after munching the raw berry.

He tried it and there the coffee habit got its start, although at first it was used as food. African tribes ground the berries, mixed the grist with fat and rolled it into balls about the size of a billiard ball. That was a man's ration for a day.

A Costly Habit

In time someone discovered how to roast and grind the berries, which then were brewed. It took many years to develop a sure-fire method of making a good cup of coffee.

My first cup was a bitter liquid poured from a pot in which the grounds accumulated from day to day. The boiled brew was made from Arbuckle's coffee, purchased in bulk for a dime a pound, and ground by the grocer.

That cup of coffee wasn't very good, and I don't know how I managed to develop a desire for the stuff.

Now, of course, I brew my coffee in a gleaming white percolator that gurgles contentedly until some inner instinct tells it the job is done. Then it shuts itself off and waits for me to pour my ration.

I never have known whether there is any food value in my coffee. Indeed, I haven't been interested enough to inquire. But I know I am hooked with a habit that costs me at the rate of $1,820 a ton. (Sept. 21, 1970)

Opportunity Taps Twice

S tories of men who unknowingly teetered on the brink of great wealth, only to let opportunity slip by, interest me as much as do tales of those who saw opportunity and made millions.

Such a man was the late Dr. W.M. Karshner, a physician I knew in a small city in Washington.

Not only once, but twice on the same day, did opportunity bang on the doctor's door.

One thing that makes the story palatable and amusing is the fact that my friend had an abiding sense of humor.

It happened soon after World War I. The young doctor was undecided about where he wanted to establish his practice. Taking "Bud" Jacobs, a young attorney friend, he set out to tour California. Maybe they would find a promising location.

They came by train. Arriving in Los Angeles, they were collared by a man representing a Long Beach subdivider. They decided to take a free ride to the beach city.

There they were taken to the sales office that was located on a barren hill at the edge of the city. They had to admit that the view was breathtaking. They could look over the shimmering sea all the way to Catalina Island. To the east and north they could see San Gabriel and the crest of Mt. Wilson.

The prices asked for tracts seemed a little high. The visitors had ready cash, but they weren't about to be taken by smooth-talking developers.

The hill that was being subdivided was Signal Hill, which the next year became one of California's wonder oil fields.

While the two men were on Signal Hill someone said they should go to a new development on the Orange County coast. There they could buy a town lot cheap. In addition they would receive an encyclopedia with the purchase.

Why not take a look? It would cost them nothing.

They took the free bus to their next stop where the developer gave them a free lunch and an upbeat lecture on the bright future of the community.

Again wary of being taken by sharpers, the doctor and his friend took a bus to Riverside to see what that city had to offer.

The beach city they rejected was Huntington Beach, soon to become another of California's fabulous oil fields.

When Riverside failed to convince them, they entrained for their homes in Washington state.

The good doctor liked to relate his experience. He seemed to have no regret. He opened a practice in his home city, became moderately wealthy, a leader in his state's medical fraternity and a University of Washington regent. At the end of his career he established a scholarship foundation for poor youths.

Jacobs, his companion on the trip, did well, too. He became a prominent attorney in his community.

Drilling for Steam

When Sportsman Well No. 2 came in, back in 1962, I was there and I took pictures of one of man's strangest natural discoveries.

It was something to see! The steam roared out across Imperial Valley waste land like nothing I ever have seen or heard.

That was one of the wells drilled by Joseph I. O'Neill, Texas oil millionaire, to test the geothermal power and chemical possibilities of the south-Salton Sea area.

His drilling stopped at 5,230 feet. At that point the earth began to gurgle and belch like a giant with a sick stomach.

It was partly by accident that I was there, even though I had planned to be on hand for the well's coming-in party. I had been waiting in San Diego for a friend to call me when the well showed signs of coming in, but he forgot.

Getting nervous lest I miss the spectacle, I decided early one morning, I think it was in February, that I'd not wait longer.

The weather was miserable. The Highway Patrol had closed Highway 80 across the Lagunas because of snow.

I packed a lunch, dressed in my warmest rough clothing, and took off for the valley about daybreak. I went by way of Campo, thinking the CHP would overlook that route. They did. There was snow, but it was not too deep for my little car.

About 10 a.m. I found the drilling rig. It was in a desolate area ordinarily used by duck hunters. A dozen or more people had gathered, none knowing what to expect. The drill had been pulled from the hole and men stood around uneasily, waiting the pressure to seep up through heavy drilling mud.

The well casing had been connected with two 8-inch pipes that led out across the desert about 100 feet.

Without warning, the well gave a mighty belch, then fell sullenly silent for a while. More belches. Steam rose from the pipes. More silence.

"She's coming in," one of the drillers shouted, and in she came! With a steady roar, escaping steam shot across the desert floor more than 100 feet from the ends of the pipes, then vanished into the clear, cool desert air.

Drillers grinned. Spectators gaped. Men with pencils and calculators began estimating the value of the well.

It would produce 5,000 KWs of electrical energy. There was a chemical output of great value, mostly bromides. There would be a great production of sodium chloride, potassium chloride, manganese, lithium, and even a measurable amount of gold. The annual output of the well might be worth $600,000.

But nothing happened after that. The chemicals produced at that location made the steam so dirty it could not be put through turbines.

I was there and I saw a dream die. A big dream. (Nov. 11, 1970)

Call of the Sea

*I*f ever I was tempted to an addiction it was by the sea. It began 15 months after my discharge from the Army at the end of World War I.

After shedding my uniform I found work as assistant engineer on a diesel-powered tug. Our chief work was towing logs on Puget Sound in the state of Washington.

It was pleasant work, not overly demanding, and it paid well. That combination may have led to my becoming enamored of the sea.

As months slipped by I realized that my affection for the life of a sailor was growing. Doubtless I was getting an addiction; if so, it had to be broken, I decided.

Supported by that thinking, I quit, and then came the full realization of what had happened to me. I sensed that I might not want to live and work ashore.

To make it possible for me to return to the sea, if I changed my mind, I took an examination to qualify me as a licensed engineer. I thus obtained a license good for five years, and renewable by going to sea for a few weeks. That was insurance, in case I found it impossible to break the habit.

I can remember to the day when I fully gave up my longing for the sea, but before that happened I never was free of the attraction of the water.

During those months I was conscious of the odor of the sea drifting over the land. The smell of a bucket of clams, the flight of a formation of ducks, the sound of a boat's whistle as it felt its way through the fog — any of these was enough to set my mind on fire.

Call of the Sea

I have gone to a theater showing a picture of a sea story and have felt the swaying of the deck under my feet. The sound of a diesel driving a boat down the channels stirred my inner longings.

For weeks after I left the boat, sleeping was a problem.

In the tug, my bunk was separated from the engine by a thin partition, and that engine was a noisy work horse. It turned over 208 times a minute, its four cylinders barking in rhythm. But when it came time for me to rest, that noise never bothered me.

Indeed, the only time I was likely to awaken was when the engine was shut down. Then the stillness awakened me.

In my self-imposed retirement, I missed that. Also I missed the food provided in our galley. I missed the wild ducks that often made our dinner, the clams and the occasional salmon we caught from the sea.

I missed the noises of the ship, the creaking of the timbers, the grinding of the powered winch bringing in the towing cable, the thumping of heavy boots on the deck.

I might have succumbed to the lure of the sea had I not met two people, a girl and a minister who said: "Repeat after me..."

A Brave Man

Pete Hawkins knew about the bad men of the Old West.

Pete was cook on a tug boat on which I served as assistant engineer following my stint with the Army in World War I.

Our cook had spent his life in the hotel kitchens of the West, but as he grew older he left that service for work that was less demanding. On our tug he seldom had to prepare meals for more than six men, including himself.

Pete was a small, pipe-smoking man with an awkward limp. As I remember him, he always wore a chef's white hat and a starched white apron when at work in the tiny galley. While ashore he dressed better than most seamen as he limped to various markets to lay in supplies for a couple of weeks.

Our tug was the envy of the tow boat crews on Puget Sound. Since we supplied our own table, his thrift was appreciated in our crew. A part of his ability to save on food bills was due to the fish we caught, the clams we dug, and the mallards, widgeon and bluebill ducks that fell before the captain's gun.

Pete never had married, although he spoke often of a sweetheart living near San Diego. He never told us her name, but he did say that she had a considerable fortune that was invested mostly in diamonds stored in a bank box.

Several years later I chanced to meet him on a Los Angeles street. His friend had suffered a disabling stoke, had sent for him and they were married only hours before she died. He inherited the diamonds.

All this is merely an introduction to Pete's experience with a bad man.

When he was 17 years old, which was around 1875, he took a job in a Butte, Mont., hotel kitchen where he was a helper. It was there that he began his training as a cook.

One day a bad man came into the kitchen with a revolver strapped to his hip, a load of gin in his belly and an evil temper. It was not uncommon for such men to emphasize their requests for personal entertainment, and knowledgeable citizens usually complied promptly.

"Dance!" he ordered, whipping out his gun. Others in the kitchen took the hint and danced. But Pete was different. He declined.

"I don't dance for anybody," he said defiantly.

Whereupon the man aimed his gun at a spot near Pete's feet and fired into the floor. Still Pete wasn't convinced.

The gun flared again and away went the toes of one of Pete's feet.

That's how Pete got his limp.

On Federal Agencies

S hould I attempt to designate the most durable of modern inventions, I would go no further than government agencies. Washington's Tea Tasters Board will illustrate.

Tea tasters are hangovers from a bygone age. Their duties pertained to determining the quality of tea imported into the Colonies before and after the Revolutionary War.

Though tea tasters no longer are required to insure the quality of tea, they have remained on the federal payroll for nearly 200 years.

I regard such agencies as phantom ships on a phantom sea, sailing for phantom ports. The crews, it should be noted, are very real people.

During World War I airplane frames were built of wood, spruce being the most desirable variety. Spruce comes from the forests of the Northwest. The wood is strong, straight-grained and free of knots.

The government needed planes to fight the Germans so it took steps to insure a ready supply of spruce lumber. An agency was set up. Men who knew about spruce were assigned the task of making sure plane builders would have plenty of material.

The war ended abruptly, but the spruce procurement agency did not. A group of men met at regular intervals for more than a quarter of a century during which, I suppose, they talked about spruce production. They met, talked, collected their fees for attending, and adjourned.

For all I know, they still may be meeting, talking about spruce, and collecting their per diem fees, although I hope not. (March 9, 1970)

Men of Mettle

A few of California's gold rush fortunes were made by men of mettle rather than by men who found glittering metal in streams that flowed from the High Sierras. They were men who relied on strength, vision and courage rather than luck.

Take the Bixby boys, Benjamin and Lewellyn, and their cousin, Dr. Thomas Flint, Maine men who had been lured to California in the early days. They were rugged individuals who knew an opportunity when they saw one, and who knew what to do about it.

The three, and another Bixby, Jotham, came to California to sample the gold fields, but they soon found the outlook bleak. One of the Bixbys worked in a butcher shop for a time and learned there the craving miners had for meat.

So the three formed a company that is known in history as Flint, Bixby & Co. They pooled their resources and converted all they owned into gold. Dividing the metal three ways, each was responsible for $3,500 which was carried in especially designed vests.

Carefully avoiding persons who might attempt to rob them, they took passage for Panama. They hiked across the isthmus, carrying their precious gold, then caught a steamer for Boston.

After visiting in their home state for a few weeks, they took a train to Illinois where they purchased 1,880 sheep. It was late winter and the sheep had not been sheared, so they took care of that, selling the wool for $1,570.

On May 7, 1853, they started a drive that was to last eight months, and that was to set them down about 2,000 miles away on land now occupied by Pasadena.

They had planned their enterprise well. In their "train" were 11 yoke of oxen, four horses, two wagons, four men besides themselves and three sheep dogs. Their wagons carried everything from cookware and blankets to spare harness and tools.

Ferrying their outfit across the Mississippi, they headed for Council Bluffs and another ferry to cross the Missouri. From there they followed the immigrant trail to Salt Lake City. It had been their intention to cross the Sierras and end the drive in Central California, but winter was coming, so they turned south.

Arriving in the Pasadena area late in December, they decided to rest and let their animals fatten on the lush winter grass. About six months later they pushed on northward toward a market for their mutton.

In the area where Hollister now is located they sold their sheep, receiving a handsome profit.

Next they decided Southern California offered more challenging opportunities. So they moved to land now occupied by Long Beach, where profits from their sheep drive enabled them to buy thousands of acres.

Oh yes, they started the drive with 1,880 sheep; they arrived with 2,400.

A Prairie Grave

A lthough I had ample warning that a little genealogy, like knowledge, is a dangerous thing, I did dip into the subject a few years ago.

My warning had been that I should not look too closely at the family tree; I just might find a horse thief hanging on one of the obscure branches.

Actually, I didn't find a horse thief, but I did find that there is no end to a genealogical record. Where does a family history begin? Where does it end?

A specific genealogy is a growing subject. It never can be closed as long as the family exists. Deaths must be recorded, marriages and births must be added to the record.

My search for facts about my family did bring up an interesting story, and it revealed yet another aspect of pioneer resourcefulness.

It happened in 1854, nearly 119 years ago, when my Aunt Aseneth died at the age of 2.

My grandparents, David and Esther McCracken, were moving from Arkansas where they had lived "one crop year." They thought they were going to Iowa. I believe the incident occurred in Kansas; a barren, wind-swept expanse inhabited by Indians, prairie dogs and wolves.

As he guided his little party across the plains, grandfather had seen two parties of Indians, one at the right and one at the left. They were keeping pace with the wagons and apparently were spying on the travelers. Thus it was impossible to stop for a simple funeral.

As night came on Grandfather pitched camp

right over the wagon wheel track he had been following. He chose a spot where the dust lay thick. As soon as it was dark he shoveled the dust aside and dug a grave.

There, under a canopy of stars, and to the strains of a prairie wolf dirge, they held a simple funeral service. Grandfather read from the family Bible and said a prayer for Aseneth, his first child, then filled the grave, compacting the soil. There was no cross or gravestone.

Over the grave he spread the dust, and next morning he drove his livestock several times over the spot. He wanted no tell-tale signs that would lead anyone to molest the burial place.

At that point in their journey my grandparents decided against Iowa. They turned eastward toward Indiana where they had been married about 1850. There they had friends and relatives and that fact probably caused them to abandon Iowa.

In Indiana they set about fulfilling the scriptural command to "be fruitful and multiply," a fact attested by my genealogical research.

Although they had 12 more children (two sets of twins), I am sure they never forgot the lonely grave on that lonely prairie roadway. (March 8, 1971)

Peavey or Cant Hook

*I*n the Pacific Northwest of yesteryear it was common to say of an individual we held in low regard:

"He can't tell the difference between a peavey and a cant hook."

That was supposed to indicate about the lowest form of dumbness. It also was supposed to measure one's own superior intellect.

Only recently have I learned that the word peavey probably should be spelled with a capital letter. It took the name of its inventor, Joseph Peavey, a lumberman who used to drive logs on Maine rivers.

One day his logs created a jam. To clear the jam, he told his blacksmith how to make a new logger's tool. It consisted of a strong handle, about five feet long. It probably was of oak.

In the end of the handle he inserted a steel spike. He then attached a swinging steel hook about 15 inches from the spike.

It turned out to be one of the best tools for loggers since the invention of the double-bitted ax. It is called a peavey.

This tool provides the grip and leverage to easily turn over a log. With it, loggers who work log rafts on the waterways of the north pry apart jams. Every logger has used one.

Joseph Peavey patented his invention, quit logging and became a manufacturer. The invention was so simple, thousands have said, "Why didn't I think of that?"

Then someone else thought the peavey could be improved. So he invented the cant hook, a tool that does most of the things a peavey can do. Take the spike from the peavey and you have a cant hook. It is used to roll a stubborn log on the ground.

The peavey is so widely used that the Joseph Peavey Co. has continued for more than a hundred years, under the same name.

Frank H. Peavey, a nephew of Joseph, also became a manufacturer. His father died when he was 9; he quit school to sell newspapers to help support his mother and his brothers and sisters. He eventually became one of the nation's great buyers and sellers of grain. He also was one of the first conglomerate operators. He manufactured grain products, ships and pianos, and operated railroads and grain elevators.

It appears he would undertake any type of honest business that could turn a profit.

Surely the Peavey family etched its name on the nation's business history. (Aug. 25, 1974)

Childhood Memories

B oys, and I suspect girls as well, miss something in life if their growing-up years leave them nothing to remember with pleasure.

I think that's true because many today are missing the sheer ecstasy of living. What did the boys of my childhood years experience that I consider worth remembering?

Not cartons of ice cream available in a half dozen flavors at any time of the day or night from the family refrigerator. Will the boy of today remember a single one of the numerous trips to the freezer?

I remember ice cream for the few times we made it in the family kitchen.

I well remember the few bunches of Fourth of July firecrackers my father bought for a nickel a bunch.

I remember the occasional day we took off in summer to go fishing in Idaho's Lolo River.

The high leather boots bought for me from a catalogue house cling to my memory. In memory I still can smell the pungent odor of new leather and the feeling of security they provided.

I remember the teacher who read with dramatic effect Longfellow's "Skeleton in Armor" at a school program, a thrilling new experience for a growing mind. It gave me a little peek at the meaning of literature.

Almost any day now a boy can hear such readings on the family TV, but will he remember a single one?

I remember the thrill of earning my first dollar. For that silver coin I walked a mile daily several weeks to care for a neighbor's poultry while he was away.

The rare experience of going to town is one I never want to forget. Our general store was filled with the ecstatic fragrance of spices, cheeses, brown sugar and spiced meat.

I have carried through life the distinctive scent of new clothing on the merchant's shelves.

The memory of my first trout, of my father's lightning-fast draw on a running deer, of the wild pursuit of two bear he had wounded, of autumn's first snow — these are not world-shattering, but where today does a boy gather such enduring memories?

Show me a boy today who remembers his first auto ride and I'll show you one in his second childhood.

I can remember the first time I tasted chewing gum. That was when I was 7 years old, and was it ever good! My share of a package was half a stick.

Such memories may seem trivial, but they are enduring. I cherish every one.

Apology To A Horse

*I*f Dick were around today I'd apologize. I'd do something meaningful to make up for the bad opinion of him I have held all these years. Maybe I'd give him an extra ration of oats, or maybe make his pallet of straw a bit softer.

The only name we had for him was Dick. In those days we didn't give our horses two names as they do now at race tracks — names like Sprightly Queen or Maud's Son.

He wasn't a big horse, tipping the scales under 1,000 pounds.

I never knew how he came to our Northern Idaho homestead. My father probably traded for him. Nor do I know when or how he left.

But I know other things about him. He was a gray gelding with a big head and small neck, and was appropriately called a knot-headed cayuse. He couldn't run very fast, but he earned his keep by helping pull a plow or by being one of the lead horses on a four-horse team.

I'd give him credit for his virtues, if he were here today.

My tendency, however, is to remember his faults. He was clumsy, but why should I hold that against him? I was no acrobat myself. He often stumbled; I often got my feet tangled in a knot.

He had an even greater fault.

Dick was what we called a night kicker. At times when he should have been sleeping, he was likely to kick with either or both hind feet. He seemed to delight in backing away as far as his tether would permit, then bang away at the barn wall. If we tied

155

him short, he would kick the walls of his stall.

Looking back now, I don't believe it was equine malice. Several times I watched him from the loft and found that he always looked around before kicking. Perhaps he really didn't want to hurt any of us.

One incident is difficult to forgive or forget. He and I fell on an icy incline. A good horse would not have fallen. And a good rider doubtless would have escaped injury.

As it was, I scrambled up the icy surface and was in the clear — that is, I was in the clear until Dick got to his feet and fell again. That's when he got me. He fell on my foot; crushing the instep.

But recently I learned that in all probability Dick suffered from arthritis. His kicking might have been his method for getting relief for his aching joints, and his clumsiness may have been the result of that malady.

Idea on the Beam

*I*t seems strange now that I should have met Dave
Gregg when and where I did. I had known him
only slightly when I was in high school.

Dave was a younger brother of Vene Gregg, a
big league baseball pitcher, and thus quite a hero in
Clarkston, Wash.

It was commonly believed that Vene was under
contract to play ball for $5,000 a year, and that was
quite a salary for playing ball for just a few months a
year. Vene tried to get Dave into baseball, but somehow he didn't make the grade.

In winter the Gregg boys and their father
worked as plasterers. I suppose most of the houses in
Clarkston had been plastered by the Gregg family. It
was a common belief that Vene's ability to throw his
fast ball came from the strong wrists developed while
using a trowel.

One winter Vene came to our school diamond
and showed the boys how he pitched. He was tall —
6 feet-3 or 4. I remember him only as an overhand,
fast-ball pitcher. When he delivered the ball he rose
high on his toes and at home plate it looked as if the
ball was literally coming from the sky.

That was the last time I ever saw Vene. I had
attended the university, taught school a couple of
years, been to war and worked on a Puget Sound tug
by the time I took a job in Chehalis, Wash. When I
learned that Dave was operating a lumber yard there I
went to see him.

Immediately he began telling me that the day
of the hand-made house was near an end. All that
was needed was a change in attitude of builders, he

said. He proposed that lumber should be cut accurately in the mill. Studding should be sawed to the exact length needed. Then the carpenter need only nail it into place, at a great saving of time and labor.

That's the way it is done today, but not the way it was done in 1921. Carpenters in those days squared off both ends of 2x4s with a hand saw.

Dave said he would reform the practice of hand-cut lumber if given a chance, but he knew how jealously workmen guarded their "rights." He didn't think they were ready to release part of their work to machines, and he wasn't about to get his nose blunted just to make sure.

As I say, I haven't seen Dave since, but I often see the effects of his idea, which now is standard American building practice.

Only it has gone farther than Dave ever dreamed.

Now, if you are building a house, not only are your studs delivered in neat ready-cut bundles, but that's the way you buy almost everything from siding and roof sheeting to laminated beams and trusses.

Golden Opportunity

I have often thought an ideal state of existence would be life beside a mound of gold from which I might withdraw at any time to buy a pocket knife, an ice cream sundae, or a new car.

Relieved of the need to work, I then could spend my days free from a hoe handle, a wheelbarrow or a typewriter. I could do exactly what I wanted to do, and I assume it would be almost nothing.

My pile of gold, of course, would not be accessible to others. They would have to work for it.

So desirable was this picture of the ideal life that I often have wandered up and down canyons and mountain sides looking for float. It did not matter that the places where I looked were the most unlikely locations for gold mines, or that prospectors already had searched the ground. Maybe they overlooked an outcrop that would rival Cripple Creek's fabulous riches.

My searching and my dreaming were futile, I am sorry to say. Such gold as I have had in my hands consisted of a few coins earned by hard work. That is still the way most gold is gleaned from the earth today.

Recently I was surprised to discover that throughout much of my life I have lived very near the earth's greatest store of the yellow metal. And I could have it now if I had the ingenuity to gather it.

This gold is in the sea, just floating around. There are billions of dollars worth of it there.

I made this discovery while reading my granddaughter's 7th grade science book.

In one cubic mile of sea water there are 440

pounds of gold. I assume these are troy weight pounds of 14 ounces each. Each ounce of gold is worth $35. Thus the gold in one cubic mile of sea water is worth $215,600. I do not know how many cubic miles of this water there are, but it would yield enough gold to choke Ft. Knox, I am sure.

It well might be that gold is not the most valuable of the minerals and salts held captive in a cubic mile of sea water.

There are in that six-sided block of water 117 million tons of salt, the text explains. I cannot imagine what I would do with so much salt, but there would be a use for some of the 283,000 tons of bromine in a cubic mile of brine. Steel makers use that stuff. My mile (I think I should file a claim on it) also contains 192 tons of iodine, six million tons of magnesium, and 5,000 tons of aluminum.

Some of these chemicals and minerals are being extracted by such operations as those of San Diego's Western Salt Co. Even a little gold is collected, but the process is too slow for me. If I can just figure out some faster method... (Nov. 30, 1962)

Frontier Bankers

Pioneers of the Old West often had to make do with what they had. They patched harness, spliced ropes, mended worn-out clothes, invented tools.

One of the strangest of frontier improvisations occurred near the turn of the century in Wardner, Idaho, a community that now is little more than weathered bits of lumber scattered over a mountainside.

Wardner, the site of the original discovery of the great silver-lead deposit that became the Bunker Hill mine, was, in its infancy, the typical mining boom town. Its homes and stores were strung along narrow streets or trails notched into the mountain wall. Nearby Milo Creek dropped swiftly to the South Fork of the Coeur d'Alene River.

Wardner was a man's town, tough as an elephant's hide. Its business was digging ore from the mountain and hauling it by mule-team 40 miles to a point where it could be picked up and carried to a smelter. Hard work, every minute of it.

There came into town two brothers who wanted a piece of the action, but mining did not appeal to them. Regardless of the fact that they had been reared in a mid-West God-fearing home, they decided to operate a gambling casino.

Business flourished. They wrote glowing accounts of their success, telling their parents they were operating a "bank." Apparently they overdid the story.

One day they received a telegram saying their parents were coming to visit them. It threw the brothers into a tizzy.

What to do?

Frontier ingenuity came to their rescue. They decided to turn their gambling hall into what looked like a regular bank. They set up a counter with teller's windows and furnished one corner with a "bank manager's" desk.

Miners, always ready to help, came to their rescue and for a week came in to make what appeared to be deposits and withdrawals. They even applied for a mock loan or two.

There was no indication that the visiting parents ever suspected. It seems probable they left Wardner filled with pride for their sons' success.

The story might end there, but it didn't. It might end with the brothers returning to the business of running a casino. But they didn't do that.

By the time I went to the community about 17 years later, Wardner had almost completely moved down Milo Creek to a site along the river and had become a new mining town — Kellogg.

The brothers had established themselves in Kellogg as owners of a highly respected bank, only this time it wasn't a faro bank. It was a place where you could get a check cashed or borrow to carry you over until next pay day.

Point of View

Nowhere in my wandering have I found people, both natives and imports, so conscious of "views" as in the Pacific Northwest.

It seems that every house must have a view. Sometimes it is only a glimpse of a mountain framed by two giant trees, but it is a view and it is cherished.

Viewing is a sedentary sport, for the most part. It can be practiced from a window, from a back porch or a front yard.

It need not be sedentary, however. There are those who fairly eat it up. They climb the highest peaks, drag boats to the most inaccessible lakes, and drive endless miles to see The Mountain from some angle not previously enjoyed.

The Mountain, incidentally, is the center of all this view worshiping, although it has its complementary features.

When you say The Mountain in the Seattle-Tacoma area you mean Mt. Rainier, which is looked upon by each native as a bit of non-transferable personal property. They speak of it quite as though each had a part in erecting this huge dorsal fin in the geological spine called the Cascades, even though the popular legend is that it was built by Paul Bunyan and Babe, his blue ox.

As a tribute to this magnificent hump of rock, ice and snow, houses are built to face it. Often fine trees are sacrificed to cut a path for the eye to reach across the 50 miles to where the sky seems to rest on its cratered crest.

Not many pause to remember the bits of history involved in majestic Mt. Rainier.

Point of View

The Mountain was discovered in 1792 by George Vancouver while he was exploring Puget Sound. He named it for Adm. Peter Rainier, ignoring the Indian name Tacoma, an act that later caused deep anguish in the city of Tacoma. The hurt now appears to have been healed.

Not until 1870 was Mt. Rainier scaled. That year Hazard Stevens and P.N. Van Trump made it to the summit. Now the more hardy climb the trail up the 14,408-foot peak each year. Last year 1,592,829 visitors were checked into Rainier National Park.

Few of those who climbed the peak, or even those who took their fun the easy way by driving to Paradise Lodge, carried away identical memories of what they saw.

Mt. Rainier offers a different view every minute of every day. This is so because the light on the 28 glaciers and the great snow fields always is changing.

For those who find their joy in lowly beauty there is, in summer, an array of flowers that stubbornly thrust their way through snow packs to reach the light.

All that, and more, is involved in the justifiable view worshiping that makes people say: "Have you seen The Mountain this morning?"

Perhaps behind all this is the ode of the Psalmist who said: "I will lift up mine eyes unto the hills, from whence cometh my help." (Sept. 1, 1962)

"Needs Love" Group

R ecently I met the qualifications for membership in a group known to me as "Needs Love." We never will pay dues and there will be no campaigns to expand membership, and no contests for office.

Most of the qualifying ritual usually takes place in a hospital, though that is not mandatory. Mine occurred mostly during 24 days. Some members spend the rest of their lives qualifying.

Those around me said I was sick, which surprised me. I know I was ill, but I didn't hurt. Most other members limped and I accepted that as a badge of membership.

For a time I felt strange as a member of this group, because of the world standing of some of the members. Jonathan Swift, British author and satirist, writer of Gulliver's Travels, became a member at age 39. He lived another 40 years.

Robert Louis Stevenson, a story teller of renown, (he wrote Treasure Island) was a member. He died of tuberculosis. Walt Whitman, the controversial poet, was a member who gained fame while wearing the credentials of "Needs Love."

The United States has had three presidents who wore the badge with honor, though the burden of membership was more than Warren G. Harding could bear. He died in office. Woodrow Wilson and Dwight D. Eisenhower completed their terms in the White House after joining the group.

I should not omit Winston Churchill, that masterful coiner of phrases who wore his badge with honor and patience.

Not that people generally expect us all to be literary geniuses or illustrious heads of state. Those who haven't made their mark before initiation are not likely to do so after joining up.

Instead, I find people ready to do our slightest bidding. I do not even have to get out of my chair all day long. I have a generous neighbor who types for me, and another who irrigates my tomatoes and fig tree. I have even ceased to be too concerned about such mundane matters as household finances. These are the rewards that go along with membership.

Besides all that, I get to sleep as long as I want, or can. When I arise after a night's rest, someone helps me get ready for breakfast and even feeds me if necessary.

Where else in all the world is there such a complete reward for belonging to a group whose greatest achievement has been to have a stroke?

The Things I Know

R ecently I wrote for this space a confession that there are things I do not know, a confession that raised a question as to what I do know, if anything.

This caused a bit of embarrassment; it has done nothing for my ego. On close examination I find convictions I once held have been abandoned, or sharply revised.

For example, I grew up under a belief that anything "as sound as a dollar" was pretty good, it was worth hanging onto. But this has to be cast aside for reasons apparent to any reader. My faith in it as a comparative has been shattered.

"Cool as a cucumber" once was, for me, a measured of composure. The individual who could remain that cool under stress was well disciplined, I thought. Later I found that cucumbers are not always cool.

"Good as gold." Who does not remember that, and especially the older generation? But what good is gold, other than to bury, as a dog buries a bone.

And I now know that anything "solid as a meetin' house" probably is suspect. Meeting houses get knocked down by earthquakes, they burn, and they sometimes are eaten by termites. As a measure of solidness they simply do not stand the test.

Similarly "hard as a rock" is an unstable simile. Rocks are not all hard. Many are soft and crumbly.

Thus I find simple values once imposed upon me were as shifting sand, and I think I know why.

These values were measures of material things. There is little in the material world that is unchanging and unchangeable. When we reach for something stable to grasp and hold we must reach beyond the material.

For instance, there is the simple matter of mature faith. Such faith is not quickly arrived at because it often is based upon reason and reasoning. This implies growth. It implies preliminary acceptance of a belief in a newly discovered truth, the abandonment of that belief when need arises, and the acceptance of another and more seasoned belief.

I know a child's warm smile is a universal antidote for lost hope.

I know a mother's love transcends the waywardness of a child; such love is not to be denied.

I know a dog's loyalty and devotion go beyond human understanding.

I know that patriotism leads men and women to lay down their lives without hesitation when need arises, and with no possibility of reward.

I know men and women give their entire lives in support of ideals, and with no thought of gaining even the hero's sobering epitaph.

Oddly enough, the things I think I know are only remotely associated with the material. I cannot touch them, but somehow they are the things that are untarnished by time. (March 15, 1963)